A Buckeye Falls Christmas

A Buckeye Falls Novella

Libby Kay

A Buckeye Falls Christmas
Copyright © 2024 Libby Kay
All rights reserved.

ISBN: (ebook) 978-1-964636-21-4
(print) 978-1-964636-22-1

Inkspell Publishing
207 Moonglow Circle #101
Murrells Inlet, SC 29576

Edited By Yezanira Venecia
Cover Art By Emily's World of Design

DEDICATION

To all the readers who fell in love with Buckeye Falls,
this is for you. ♥

CHAPTER 1
Kibble wars and holiday plans

"Max!" Ginny shouted her husband's name from the kitchen, where she was elbow-deep in dog food. "You got a minute?" she asked as she attempted to tidy up the pile of spilled kibble. Meanwhile, their rescue dog, Zippy, scarfed down every morsel he could get. Their son, Henry, found the whole scene hilarious, considering he was the cause of the chaos.

"Look at Zippy's tail," the young boy exclaimed, clapping from his perch on the counter. "It's going a million miles an hour." He slapped his forehead and cried, "I should be filming this."

"Holy crap," Max exclaimed when he joined the fray. His salt-and-pepper hair was still wet from the shower, curling at his temples. Ginny lamented that she wouldn't get to enjoy a moment with her husband, as she adored the smell of his skin fresh out of the shower. Max crunched over to the hound and grabbed Zippy's collar. "All right, buddy. Let's go."

As soon as Max opened the back door, Zippy sprinted outside and barfed in the grass, much to the delight of Henry. "Awesome!"

Ginny slumped against the stove and huffed out a laugh. "That was like, fifty bucks of kibble he just tossed."

Max walked to the counter, scooped up their son, and plopped him down on the floor. "Good news, Hen," he said, striving to keep his smile at bay. "You get to do two chores before school today." Max waggled two fingers in front of his son.

Henry rolled his eyes and looked more like his older sister, who was dangerously close to her teens. "Dad, I'll be late."

Ginny joined them at the counter, thrusting a dustpan and broom at the men in her life. "Should have thought of that before you decided to play kibble wars with Zippy." She winked at Max and went to work making coffee. Her morning routine had been sadly interrupted when she'd discovered Henry upending the dog food canister onto the floor and setting the kitchen timer.

"Otis said their dog ate a whole bag in five minutes," he'd declared over his shoulder, clearly undeterred by his mother's reaction. "I said Zippy could whoop his butt."

By the time Ginny had cornered the poor dog, his snout was covered in kibble dust. While she loved Otis, her best friend's son had become a bit of a role model for Henry. It was great he had friends in his corner, but she could have done without the literal double dog dare unfolding in her kitchen. "Remind me to thank Natalie for this little challenge."

Max pushed Henry toward the mess and looped his arm around his wife's waist, pulling her flush against him. Even after fifteen years, he savored every chance to touch Ginny. Their life was busier than ever, but they still made time for each other. Although lately, not nearly as much as he wanted.

Ginny leaned into Max's embrace and kissed his cheek before groaning at the time. "Crap on a cracker." She sighed and stepped back, glancing at her smartwatch. "Shouldn't Josie be pestering us for breakfast already?"

Henry tossed his head back and bellowed his sister's name so loudly, the walls shook. "Good Lord, Hen," Max said, covering his ears. "What did we say about yelling in the house?" The young boy merely shrugged and went back to shoveling dog food back into the bin.

"Um, ewww." Their daughter announced from the doorway. She was the spitting image of her mother. Josie's reddish-brown hair hung down by her shoulders, and she wore one of Ginny's old red sweaters. "Why is Zippy barfing all over the yard?"

Her brother spun on his heels and triumphantly held up the empty dustpan. "Great news!" he beamed, pushing past his parents to get in his sister's face. "Zippy ate over half a bag of kibble before Mom ruined it."

Josie wrinkled her nose and shuddered, already looking like a teenager much to her parent's chagrin. "I'm not cleaning that up," she said after gagging.

Max ruffled Henry's hair and chuckled. "You're right, Josie. Your brother is—right now, so I can make breakfast."

Ginny patted her daughter's shoulder before pouring a cup of coffee. Her feet crunched down on a pile of kibble, and she winced. "Hen, come on. You need to clean this up before we let Zippy back inside." Judging from the unholy sounds coming from their yard, it wouldn't be anytime soon. Glancing back at the time, she winced. "We're so late already. I cannot wait for Christmas break."

Max snorted a laugh. "Because we're so ready to host our friends and already bought all our presents?"

Not only was Christmas a week away, but the Sanchez clan was hosting. Despite co-owning an events business, Ginny was woefully behind on the details. "Don't remind me. I need to check with Natalie about what they're doing. Fortunately, it sounds like Alice and James will have some free time to lend a hand."

Max cracked a carton of eggs into a bowl and started whisking. "Are he and Alice back from New York?" He tossed a pat of butter into a frying pan before snapping his fingers at Henry. "Hen, you missed a pile over here."

Ginny added cream to Max's mug before sliding his caffeine across the counter. "I think they got back this morning, but don't quote me on that." She took a sip from her cup before adding, "Or they might have been in Canada? You know those two, I never know where they're jet setting to next."

Josie paused her texting long enough to glance up at her mother. "Do you think we'll get to go to New York again in the new year?"

Ginny smiled at her daughter. "I hope so. We had so much fun with Alice last year." Alice had joined her husband in the Big Apple for an art show in the spring. She decided to host a girl's weekend for all her Buckeye Falls ladies who could get away. It had been amazing, palling around the city with her daughter, showing her places she'd loved while she was a temporary New Yorker. Natalie had brought her daughter Madeline, and Mallory and CeCe had made it as well, rounding out their friend group.

"No peppers in my eggs, Dad," Josie said, already with her nose back in her phone.

Max bit his lip. "I know, honey. This isn't my first time making you breakfast."

Finally finished with his kibble clean-up, Henry joined his sister at the table and sighed. "Are we having bacon?"

"No time," Max replied, scooping out cheesy scrambled eggs for his family. Henry's plate was covered in diced peppers and ham, while Josie's plate was a sunny pile of frill-free eggs.

Both children dug into their breakfasts without a word, earning a reminder from Ginny. "What do we say when someone slaves away over a meal for us?"

"Dad does this for a living," Josie said. "Like, all over town." She flapped her arms around her, as if her father fed all of Buckeye Falls. *Well, he kind of did.*

Ginny stifled a groan. "Yes, Dad is a chef, but he's not on the clock. What do we say?" She raised an eyebrow at her children. Through a mouthful of eggs, they mumbled "Thanks."

Yes, Max was a chef, but he had also started a restaurant empire in Buckeye Falls. Not only did he own the only diner in town, but he and CeCe and Evan had a successful side hustle with their food truck, yet Max wasn't done expanding. His newest restaurant, Max's Gin Joint, was set to open after the diner's renovations began. It was the first time he'd own a place with a liquor license, specializing in higher-class fare. The new place was also a way for him, CeCe, and Evan to stretch their culinary muscle.

Max had poured his heart and soul into the diner, but the old girl needed a facelift. The kitchen was out of date, the booths were lumpier than cozy, and the steps outside were bordering on a liability. This Christmas meal would be the last in the space, and Max wanted to say goodbye in style—with his dearest friends.

At Ginny's insistence, they invited everyone they loved for Christmas dinner. It would be a potluck affair with their best friends and all the kids. Most everyone's parents were traveling for the holiday this year, so the friends looked forward to an intimate celebration. Max's fingers itched with the need to cook something fabulous; the necessity to feed his favorite people something truly festive and over the top.

Max's musings were interrupted by a wailing sound from the backyard. Henry was on his feet in seconds, dashing out the backdoor before Ginny could even put her fork down. "Wait!" she shouted as she clambered to her feet, Josie followed right behind her.

Max was faster, pushing outside just in time to see Henry carry Zippy in his arms. The young boy's lips trembled as he cradled the dog to his chest. "Z ... Z..." his words faltered, stopping Max dead in his tracks. Opening his mouth again, nothing came out but a whimper.

When they'd had their children, all Max prayed for was healthy kids. He'd begged the universe to spare his children from the pain of a stammer, from the embarrassment of needing to find their words. He'd dealt with his fumbling tongue his whole life, and despite gaining confidence over the years, he knew it was draining for Henry.

It was almost as if his mouth was too quick for his brain, desperate to spew out every thought all at once, causing the letters to tumble together into alphabet soup. During his childhood, the stutter made Max a popular target for bullies. The one person who never wavered with patience and kindness with his infernal stammer was Ginny. When they'd met in high school, she'd never giggled or rolled her eyes, instead choosing to wait while he found his words … and in some ways found himself.

Yet there were circumstances where time didn't heal all wounds. Watching his son struggle brought a lump to Max's throat, and he stuttered as he fell to his knees and took Zippy from Henry's shaking grasp. His throat was dry, constricting against the anguish. "Z … Z … Zippy will b … be okay." He held up the dog's front paw and saw a nail embedded in the pad.

Ginny was at Max's side, rubbing her hand up and down his back in soothing circles. "Looks like he stepped on a nail, but it'll be okay." Turning over her shoulder, Ginny found Josie waiting. Her sullen pre-teen expression evaporated; the girl's eyes were the size of hubcaps. "Call Gramps, and tell him to swing by with the crate for Zippy. I'm taking him to the vet on my way to work."

Josie nodded and dashed inside.

Max dipped his head; his tongue as heavy as a cinder block, a dark curl falling over his forehead. "Th … thanks."

Ginny pressed a kiss to Max's temple, whispering words of encouragement as his heart rate slowed. "You're both just a little excited," she cooed. "It's okay."

Henry wiped at his eyes with his sleeve. "Will Zippy be all right?" he asked, his speech recovering quickly.

Ginny nodded, reaching out to smooth back his cowlick. Much like his father, Henry's hair loved to curl in every direction.

"Zippy is fine. Gramps will be here soon, and we'll get him all sorted out."

No sooner had Ginny uttered the words, her father, Harold, bounded outside with the crate and his wife, Mona, hot on his heels.

Mona was clad in one of her signature Christmas ensembles. This sweater was green with red handprints all over and flashing lights the colors of cranberries. Josie and Henry had made it years ago, and Mona wore it every chance she got as soon as the Halloween sweaters were packed away for the season.

"We got here as fast as we could," Mona gasped as she helped Harold with the crate. Max lifted the dog inside, muttering words of reassurance as they closed the door. Zippy sneezed and curled up in the crate, seemingly resigned to his impending vet visit.

Josie came outside holding her brother's coat. "Hen, the bus will be here any second." Her hands trembled as she shook the garment in his direction.

Henry hugged Max and Ginny before following his sister inside.

Max ran a hand down his face and stood. "Thanks for saving the day," he said to his in-laws.

Harold patted his shoulder and nodded. "I'm just glad we were driving by when Josie called. We're on our way to pickleball at the community center, but we'll drop Zippy off on the way."

Ginny hugged her step-mother and sighed. "You're both lifesavers."

Mona shook her head. "We're family. It's nothing. Now, you two take a moment to calm down. I'll make sure they get on the bus." She turned and headed back into the house, humming *Jingle Bell Rock* under her breath.

Harold shared another round of hugs before sidestepping a pile of Zippy's puke. Pointing with his toe, he frowned. "Do I want to know?"

Ginny snorted with laughter. "You might want to tell

Dr. Fredericks that Zippy took part in the Buckeye Falls dog food eating competition."

Harold raised an eyebrow but didn't argue. "I have a feeling the Snyder boy put him up to it."

"History repeating itself," Max said with a chuckle. While hardly hell raisers, he and Anthony got into some trouble back in the day. "Be sure to send the bill to Representative Snyder's office." He winked and Harold guffawed.

Once the house was empty, Ginny took Max's hand and pulled him to the living room. They collapsed onto the couch, both still buzzing from the morning's excitement. Ginny held one of Max's hands in hers, squeezing it tight. "This has to be a record."

"What does?"

"Two pet emergencies in one hour."

Max grimaced. "Poor Zippy."

"He'll be okay." Ginny nudged Max with her elbow. "Will you be?"

Sighing, he pulled Ginny close, draping his arm around her shoulder. "It breaks my heart," he said, nearly choking on the last word. "Hen shouldn't have to deal with a freaking stammer."

Ginny kissed his cheek, tasting his tears on her lips. "Max, honey. This rarely happens. Hen's teachers said they seldom hear it in school, and he's never complained. C'mon, he's going to be the lead in the Christmas pageant. He's a tough kid, just like his father." She punctuated her statement with another kiss.

Max coughed and wiped his eyes with the back of his hand. "Oh yeah, I'm a real macho man."

"Yeah, because you know they're my type." She theatrically rolled her eyes.

"I shudder to think of what your type is," Max said, gesturing at his current state. His eyes were red, he was covered in dirt and kibble, and he probably could stand another few hours of sleep.

Ginny leaned back, tapping her chin. "Well, let's see. I like a man who can take care of me and my children. Someone who can cook, like really well. And it would be nice if he was a small business owner and took care of my father like his own. Oh, and if he's also best friends with my best friends, that would be perfect." Ginny huffed and pulled herself to her feet. "Looks like that's a pretty tall order."

Max snatched Ginny's hand and pulled her onto his lap. "Okay, Mrs. Sanchez. Point made." He kissed his wife, relishing in the fact they were still together after all these years. Life wasn't always perfect, but it was from where he sat.

"I need to get to the diner and start working on the menu for Christmas."

Ginny kissed him one more time before pulling back. "And I'm needed in the office, but I'll swing by the vet on my way in."

"Love you, Gin."

"Love you more."

CHAPTER 2
Pancakes, baby bumps, and sibling bonding

"I love you to pieces," CeCe said through clenched teeth, "but if you don't step away from the stove, I'm going to hit you with this whisk." She brandished the utensil like a sword, jabbing it into the air.

Evan held his hands up in surrender, but he didn't move out of the way. "Not gonna happen, babe. The doctor said you're on bed rest. Don't make me call Max."

His wife shot daggers at him before turning her attention back to her batter. "The babies want pancakes, and I want to make them."

With a huff, Evan placed his hands on CeCe's hips and attempted to push her out of the way. A few months ago, this would not have been a challenge, but that was before she'd expanded to fit their growing family. Not only was Evan delighted at his wife's transformation, but he was also jubilant to meet his children in the new year. CeCe was just as excited, but she was also the vehicle for their twins and didn't like being told what to do.

"Need I remind you, I'm perfectly willing and able to make pancakes."

CeCe poked Evan's bicep. "I don't want Bisquick."

Evan covered his heart with his hand, jaw falling to the floor. "Woman, you wound me. When was the last time I made you anything from a box?"

CeCe cocked her head and tapped her temple. "That one time after we moved in together." She winced. "I'm pretty sure you even used butter from a tub."

"That was like eight years ago," Evan deadpanned, already pulling out eggs and milk from the fridge. "Not to mention, we've won several food competitions and helped open a new restaurant since then. I'm pretty sure I can handle a little pancake batter."

Quirking an eyebrow, CeCe relented and handed the bowl and whisk to her husband. "All right, tough guy. Show me what you've got."

Evan slid the bowl away before flexing his hands and lowering his voice. "I intend to." Cradling CeCe's head, Evan pulled her close for a searing kiss. Their bickering ceased as they melted against each other, lost in the moment, breakfast forgotten.

"Eww, gross," Mallory said as she entered the room, weighed down by a baby carrier, an exhausted expression on her face. Her brown hair was pulled into a messy braid, her cheeks rosy from the Ohio winter air.

Behind her, in the doorway, her husband, Beckett, shouted, "Yo! Lawless! A little help."

Evan leaned in to kiss CeCe on the forehead and whispered, "To be continued on the pancakes and everything these hands can do." Turning to his sister, he said, "You know that key was just for emergencies." He was all talk though, and gladly welcomed his sister and best friend into their home.

Mallory handed the carrier to Evan and huffed. "This is an emergency. I'm about to pee my pants."

CeCe frowned, rubbing her belly. "I thought those types of emergencies ended when the baby arrived."

Mallory snorted but recovered quickly. "Oh, CeCe, we need to talk more." She linked her arm through CeCe's and yanked her in the direction of the bathroom. "Let me pee, and then I'll fill you in on the wonders your body can do."

As the women made their exit, Evan pulled his newest niece out of her carrier. "God, Foxy. She keeps getting cuter and cuter." Evan carefully swiped a red lock of hair off Maybelle's tiny forehead. His heart clenched as she let out a sigh and fell back to sleep. "She looks just like you, man."

Beckett flinched and checked the hallway. "Don't let Mal hear you say that. She's still waiting for Maybelle's hair to turn dark." Lowering his voice, he added, "Which I don't think is going to happen." Walking over to the box he dropped by the door, Beckett kicked the side. "These are the decorations for the Christmas dinner. Please tell Max we're willing to help with whatever he needs. It's just nice they want to include Mal, me, and the baby."

Evan sighed, a long exhale that was more theatrical than useful. "And how many times do I need to tell you to relax and let this town love you? You're family, Foxy. Now cut the crap and help me make pancakes. The babies are hungry, and my wife is a little scary this morning."

Beckett strode to the sink and washed his hands. "Yeah, but you like it."

Evan cracked another egg into the batter and beamed. "No, I don't. I freaking *love* it." His infectious smile grew tenfold when his wife and sister joined them. CeCe wasted no time pulling Maybelle into her arms.

"Look how big she's getting." She clasped the baby to her chest, her eyes misting over. "I just hope our kids and Maybelle are best friends. The thought is literally keeping me up at night." She sniffled, bottom lip trembling. "I feel like they will be, right? Their fathers are best friends, Mal and I are best friends, and we're family. It's like the trifecta of love, right?"

Behind her shoulder, Evan mouthed "Trifecta of love?" before Beckett shook his head.

Mallory yanked a tissue from her pocket and handed it to CeCe, then glared at her brother. One of the biggest changes to the pastry chef was not the weight gain or newfound love of anything related to batter, but her quickness to cry. Whether it was a car insurance commercial or a sweet gesture from her husband, CeCe would be in tears within seconds if the wind blew the wrong way.

"Babe, you're right," Evan insisted from his side of the kitchen, "they're going to be besties for life. They're half Foxy and half Lawless. C'mon!"

Mallory balled up a napkin and tossed it at her brother. "Gross. Maybelle is clearly half *Lawson,* not yours," she chided, referring to Beckett's nickname for her very law-abiding little brother.

CeCe groaned and rubbed the small of her back. Beckett took Maybelle and hoisted her onto his hip. "You want to have a seat, CeCe? I'll make sure Ev doesn't burn breakfast."

Mallory, always ready to play nurse off the clock, looped her hand through CeCe's and drug her sister-in-law to the sofa. "I'm fine," she whined as Mallory placed a pillow at her back and positioned her feet onto the coffee table. "I want my Maybelle time."

"That girl isn't going anywhere," Mallory promised as she fell onto her own cushion. "How are you feeling?" She studied CeCe another moment, and asked, "For real."

CeCe rested her hands on her belly, rubbing circles over the bulge. Through an enormous grin, she recited her symptoms. "Exhausted, bloated, hangry, gassy, and very excited."

"All reasonable feelings and symptoms." Mallory winked. "How much longer?" Her head fell back on the couch as CeCe counted.

"One month, one week, and three days. I've lost track of how many hours …" she said with a huff. "Although, to be fair, I've lost track of a lot lately." Wiggling her toes, she laughed. "I can't remember the last time I saw my feet. Although I can still tie my own shoes."

Mallory nodded sagely. "Welcome to pregnancy brain.

In addition to having to pee all the time, you're also going to forget eighty percent of what you need to remember." Jostling her own legs, she huffed. "And the jury is out on when you'll see your feet again."

"You'd think I would be better prepared," CeCe said. "It's certainly taken long enough to get here." She trailed squiggles over her baby bump with her finger, her eyes glistening, bottom lip trembling.

It hadn't been an easy road to baby for Evan and CeCe. Due to some unforeseen health ailments, it took them over six years to conceive the twins. Unfortunately, they had two miscarriages along the way. Mallory had grieved alongside her brother and sister-in-law, all the while battling with guilt that Maybelle had come along relatively easily.

In contrast, Beckett and Mallory's road to baby was delayed on purpose. After taking far too long to find each other again, the pair enjoyed their newlywed phase in peace on the apple farm. As the years rolled by, Mallory had craved more of a challenge at work, so she'd gone back to school to become a nurse practitioner. During the sleepless nights of studying for exams, Beckett had taken the time to hire more crew for the farm and turned it into the destination it was today.

The Lawsons and Foxes had certainly been busy, but now was time to celebrate and relax together.

"These twins are strong and healthy. Evan showed me the results of your checkup last week. You're all going to be fine." She squeezed CeCe's arm and offered her most reassuring nurse smile.

"Breakfast is ready!" Evan yelled from the kitchen. "How many pancakes do you ladies need?"

Beckett carried a sleeping Maybelle in her carrier. "I'll bring in some coffee, Mal. CeCe, what do you need?"

"A latte and a shot of bourbon," she lamented. "But I guess orange juice is fine, too."

"Coming right up." Beckett jogged to the kitchen and came back out with Evan and a tray of food. "Ladies," he said as he handed each of them a plate of pancakes.

CeCe eyed Evan as she took her first bite, which was swimming in butter and syrup like she liked. After swallowing she nodded. "These aren't bad."

Mallory covered her mouth and moaned. "Holy crap, Ev. These are sinful. What did you do?"

Evan sent his sister a withering look before replying, "It's just Bisquik."

CeCe shot him a lewd gesture before devouring her pancakes in sixty seconds. Ever the dutiful husband, Evan swapped his wife's empty plate for his full one. "Thank you," she muttered in between mouthfuls.

Maybelle slept through breakfast, much to her parent's delight. "Wow," Beckett whispered as they cleared the dishes. "I don't think we've shared a meal without interruption in five months."

"Shhh, you'll jinx it." Mallory hissed, poking her husband in the ribs.

When everyone was back in the kitchen, CeCe pulled herself onto a stool and rested her elbows on the counter. "While we're all here, and before the Christmas insanity begins, I wanted to talk about Beck's Bakery."

Beck's Bakery was the new shop built on Beckett and Mallory's property. They lived on his late grandfather's apple farm, and had gone into business with CeCe and Evan for the bakery, building it at the entrance to the orchards for the high season.

Mallory shot her husband a look before answering. "We've been talking about that, actually. How do you feel about pushing the opening back until the following year?"

CeCe blinked. "But we're all set to open this summer, right before the fall festivities start."

Evan rested a hand on his wife's shoulder and squeezed. "Babe, maybe Mal's right. We could give it a year while we get settled in with the twins."

CeCe was incredulous. "I can do it," she pressed, "I can do it all. Just because I'm a mother doesn't mean I won't be a pastry chef, too."

Mallory covered CeCe's hand with her own and squeezed. "I have no doubt, but you're going to have two babies. I can barely handle my workload at the hospital with Maybelle."

Beckett raised his hand and added, "And I work a lot less than Lawless." A few years ago, Beckett had left his job in finance to take over the operations of the family farm. There was only a small flock of sheep and the apple orchards, but it was a full-time job keeping it running.

During the high season two years ago, visitors praised the pastries they bought at the gift shop. CeCe and Evan had a side hustle going out of the diner on weekends where they'd bake pies and cookies for Beckett's farm, but after they kept selling out, they decided to open a pop-up shop on the property. That was all before they got pregnant with the twins, and reality was starting to settle in.

"We just don't want you to overdo it, babe." Evan kissed the top of CeCe's head.

Mallory stifled her grin. "Although, we know you're going to."

CeCe shook her head and sighed. "Please don't make any decisions now, okay? Let's see how we're doing when the babies arrive."

Beckett looked to Mallory and nodded. "That sounds like a good idea." Pushing his glasses back up his nose, he asked the question everyone wanted to know. "Have you guys picked out names yet?"

LIBBY KAY

CHAPTER 3
Political and creative ambitions for the win

"Aunt Alice, let me help." Madeline snatched the suitcase from Alice's grip and led the way to the exit. The Columbus Airport was busier than usual with the pre-Christmas rush, and James had to hold Alice's hand so she wasn't swallowed up by the growing crowds.

"And you drove here all by yourself?" Alice asked for the third time in as many minutes. Granted, it had been nearly three months since she'd laid eyes on her niece, but it still didn't seem fathomable that Maddie was driving—alone.

Madeline hoisted Alice's suitcase into the trunk of her car before turning to James and offering to help. "I've got it, Maddie. Thanks." James easily lifted their last case into the trunk and closed the hatch. "We really appreciate you picking us up. It's been a long week."

"Happy to help. Plus, it gave me a break from Mom and Grandma's drama." She rolled her eyes and unlocked the car with her key fob. "Even while on a cruise, Grandma can be a pain in the butt."

Alice gave James the passenger's seat so he could spread out, but she sat in the middle of the back. Leaning on the edge of the seat, she asked, "And Anthony knows you're here picking us up? Alone? During rush hour traffic in a major metropolitan area."

Madeline let out a very unladylike snort as she put the car in reverse and headed toward the parking garage exit. "Nope. I knocked him over the head with a pipe and tied him up in the garage. He won't know we're gone for another twenty minutes."

Alice huffed out a laugh at her niece's sense of humor. "Are you sure you're not my child?" She patted Maddie's shoulder before finally resting back in her seat.

From the passenger's seat, James frantically replied to texts and emails that he missed during their flight home from Canada. His most recent show was a huge hit in Toronto, so he and Alice rented an apartment downtown while his new pieces were shown. It was times like that, nestled together in an Airbnb with her husband watching the city outside drift by, that Alice was grateful for their nomadic lifestyle and careers.

She had just signed a contract for her third book of essays with her new publisher, and she had a regular by-line at a travel magazine. She wrote about their travels, the people they met, and most importantly the food they ate. While she would clack away on her laptop, James would be splattered in paint or sanding large pieces of wood. Their creative jobs were not for everyone, but they fit them both perfectly.

Madeline pulled onto the highway and turned on the radio. Taylor Swift blared around them until James tactfully turned it down and turned in his seat. "So, Maddie, how's school? You're a junior now, right?"

Much to Alice's delight and relief, her niece seamlessly merged across three lanes of traffic and headed in the direction of home. After a decade, it still felt foreign for Alice to think of Buckeye Falls as home, but it truly was. Even with all their travels, she and James both craved the familiarity and comfort of their house. It was their space, and it was surrounded by their friends and family. Buckeye Falls had their hearts.

As the holidays approached, they pondered visiting his parents while they were traveling in South Korea, but the pull to a cozy midwestern Christmas was too strong. The forecast teased hints of the white stuff, and Alice relished the prospect of cozy nights at home with her husband. Plus, Max and Ginny hosting at the diner that had created some of her favorite meals was too good to be true.

The quirky diner held a lot of fond memories for Alice and her inner circle. Not only had her brother and sister-in-law renewed their wedding vows there, but it was the site of her first dates with James. They fell in love in the old place, and she wanted to pay her respects. And maybe eat a few cheesy bites …

Lost in her musings, she missed James's question. "Did you hear me, honey?" His dark eyes flashed as she shook herself back to the moment. "Do you want Maddie to take us home first, or to your brother's?"

Alice looked down at her worn outfit and shrugged. "Anthony and Nat have seen worse than this. Let's say hi before we crash."

James winked and turned back to their niece. "You heard the lady. Take us to casa de Snyder."

Madeline shot a thumbs-up before going back to her conversation about her art classes in school. It wasn't that she wasn't into arts as a child, but under the helpful instructions of her uncle, Madeline took to art like a fish to water. She'd had three pieces on display at the high school shows already, all before her senior year.

They arrived at Anthony and Natalie's house just as Alice ran a brush through her hair. James opened the door, held out a hand, and led her into the backdoor. Before they could cross the threshold, Otis flung the kitchen door open and barreled into them. He'd had yet another growth spurt since they'd seen him, and he looked older than his thirteen years.

"Hey man," James said, ruffling Otis's dark hair as he hugged Alice.

"I missed you guys. It's been so boring around here." Otis pulled back, looking around for his sister. "Did Maddie crash into anything?"

"I heard that, asshole." She spat from behind them.

"Language, kids. My poor ears." Alice stuck her tongue out at Madeline, who paid for her beater car with the money from her childhood swear jars. "I'm guessing now that you're driving, you have no need to be the profanity police."

"Boy, it has been a while," her brother said as he strode into the kitchen. While a little tired from a long day at work, his smile was genuine and warmed her heart.

"Tony!" Alice teased, shelling out his least favorite nickname and falling back into the familiar little sister role. They may be in their forties, but she was never too old to harass her brother.

James shook Anthony's hand before sidestepping to hug Natalie. "Thanks so much for having Maddie pick us up. You guys are lifesavers."

Natalie beamed and pulled James into a warm embrace. "Are you kidding? What's the point of having children of driving age if you can't use them for personal laziness?" She stepped back and looked over his shoulder for Alice. "Now I've seen the world-famous James Gibson. Where is future best-selling author Alice Snyder-Gibson?" She craned her neck as if the room was crawling with authors.

"Oh, I didn't realize we were throwing around titles." Alice yanked Natalie closer and threw her arms around her neck. She took a deep breath and savored the aroma of her sister-in-law's lemony shampoo. No matter the time of year, Natalie always smelled like a citrus grove.

James chuckled. "Yeah, good point. Should we call you Representative Snyder now?" he asked Anthony, who blushed as he busied himself opening a bottle of wine.

"Not until the inauguration next month, and that's only if you're in trouble." He winked and popped the cork, the sound echoing in the crowded kitchen. "Everyone drinking?" he asked, gesturing to his sister with the corkscrew.

"Yes, please." Madeline raised her hand and smiled. It was the grin that usually had her father eating out of her hand, but not in matters of booze.

Anthony opened the fridge and grabbed two cans of pop. "Nice try, yet again."

Maddie took the drinks, handed one to Otis, and shrugged. "Can't blame a girl for trying." She and Otis clinked cans, muttering something to each other before they stalked out of the kitchen.

Alice felt rooted in place, watching the children she used to crawl around and play with become real people. Madeline's blonde pigtails were now soft curls that looked just like her mother's. Otis had grown from chubby toddler to gangly pre-teen overnight, his dark hair curling at his ears like his father's. If she wasn't certain it was present day, Alice would swear she was back in their childhood home.

"So, tell us all about Canada. Did you see Justin Trudeau? I hear he's still single." Natalie waggled her eyebrows as she sipped from her wine glass.

Alice snorted. "You realize we're both happily married, right? And now that Anthony's a big-shot politician, wouldn't he have a connection to the handsome former PM?"

Anthony grumbled while he pulled out pots and pans for dinner. He was still dressed for work in a suit, the tie loosened around his neck. "I'm a state representative, Alice. I won't be making weekly trips to our neighbors to the north for parliament meetings."

Alice pointed at her brother. "Not with that attitude you won't."

James came up behind her and snaked his arms around her waist, pulling her against his frame. Just like two puzzle pieces, she clicked into place and sighed contentedly. Even after nearly a decade of marriage, Alice still got weak in the knees for her husband.

"If you're trying to make your husband jealous, you're succeeding," he teased, nuzzling her neck and whispering things that should not be shared in her brother's kitchen.

Natalie gushed, covering her heart with her hands. "You two are still so freaking sweet. I love it."

Alice smiled, enjoying the moment of domestic bliss with her family. It felt like yesterday that they all stood in this very same spot; she and James figuring out their relationship, her brother and Natalie doing the same.

Now it all felt perfect, like a Norman Rockwell painting come to life. Anthony threw an apron on, rolled up his sleeves, and started dicing onions and root vegetables. James washed his hands and joined his brother-in-law, discussing the holidays and plans for the new year. Natalie preheated the oven before joining Alice at the counter, wine bottle in tow.

"Top off?" she asked, pouring without waiting for an answer.

"I won't say no. There's no jet lag, thank God." They clinked glasses and immediately fell back into their old rapport. "So, how's N&G?"

The events business Natalie ran with Ginny had celebrated its tenth anniversary earlier that year. At the beginning, Alice worked as their assistant, but very quickly everyone outgrew that arrangement. "Busy and fabulous," Natalie replied, slurping from her glass. "Ginny and I hired another planner last month and an assistant, so that takes us to seven employees. Our territory covers all of Ohio and a few places in Indiana and Michigan."

Alice spluttered with her wine. "Are you serious? Nat, that's freaking amazing." Reaching out, she took Natalie's hand and squeezed. "You must be so relieved."

Natalie nodded, her diamond earrings swaying with the movement. "Oh yeah. Once Anthony started campaigning, I knew I couldn't do it all without more help. Ginny's busy with the kids and Max, so it only made sense." Placing her glass down, she flapped her hands and added, "Enough about me. I want to hear about everything. Toronto. Your new book contract, and whatever else you two lovebirds got into."

Alice smiled, relishing the sensation of gabbing with one of her favorite people. "Well, I guess a lot has happened," she started, knowing that was an understatement.

While she poured out all the updates to their lives, Alice missed the other people in her Buckeye Falls orbit. She had plans to see Mallory soon, least of all to see her friend's new baby. It had been months since she laid eyes on little Maybelle. Unlike her previous visits back to Buckeye Falls, Alice thought she might have missed more than she bargained for.

LIBBY KAY

CHAPTER 4
Deck the Halls

"Are you sure we can't help with decorations?" James asked Max, who balanced precariously on a ladder in the diner's dining room.

Alice piped up next to her husband. "I mean, it's kind of our thing." She smirked, referencing Buckeye Falls' fall festival and how they met.

Max chuckled, reaching out to clip a length of garland over the counter. "These are great, seriously. Evan dropped off some decorations from Beckett's farm, so we're all set." He added one more tack to the wall before coming off the ladder. "You guys hungry?"

Alice nodded, patting her stomach. "Yes. Is my favorite waitress working today?"

"Only until the end of the week. When this place closes for renovations, I'm retiring," Helen said, emerging from the kitchen with a tray of drinks. She was clad in her uniform, smirk firmly in place. "Have a seat, kids. I'll be right with you."

"What?" Alice's jaw dropped as James helped her to a booth. Max followed them with a pair of menus. "Helen can't retire. She just can't."

James patted his wife's hand as he slid into his side of the booth. "Alice, I'm pretty sure it's a free country."

Max tapped on the front of the menu where the daily special was written. "I'm not about to tell you how old she is, but let's just say it's time." Turning to Alice, he asked, "Ginger ale?"

"Yes, please. Although I might need something stronger to get over the shock."

Helen appeared at the table, two ginger ales at the ready. "Oh calm down, kid. You knew the day was coming." She slid their glasses across the table and put her hands on her hips. "I'm approximately three hundred years old, and eventually I'd like to put my feet up."

"But no one takes care of us like you do, Helen," Alice protested, swigging from her drink.

Helen leaned in and winked. "Don't tell anyone, but there are these people called waitresses. Max can hire someone a third my age and you'll get your meals before they've had a chance to cool."

"Well, I'm still going to pout about it." Alice stuck her tongue out and fell back in her seat. James covered his grin with his menu, intent on avoiding his wife's mood.

"Pout all you want, kid. I'm looking forward to enjoying my golden years without being on my feet and using Icy Hot all the damned time." Helen stretched her back and the sound of her bones popping echoed throughout the dining room. James couldn't hide his grimace.

Alice slapped her menu closed and crossed her arms. "But who will take care of us when we're here? No one knows how I like my eggs or how James like his..." She trailed off, the wind leaving her sails.

James lifted an eyebrow and suggested, "Steak?"

"Yes! How James likes his steaks." Alice snapped her fingers triumphantly.

Helen muttered something under her breath and tucked her pencil behind her ear. "Over easy and medium rare."

Alice pointed at the older woman, and said, "This is why

we need you."

Helen leaned in again, and whispered, "Just pretend you're at any other restaurant the next time you're back. I'm guessing most waitresses don't memorize every patron's order."

"Exactly! That's why we come here." Alice slapped her hand on the tabletop.

"I thought you came here for the fabulous food and time with your bestie," Mallory quipped from behind Helen. She was clad in winter gear, pair of braids spilling out from under her wool cap. Maybelle was tucked against her chest, her plump cheeks rosy from the cold.

The sound Alice emitted could have broken glass. Helen winced and backed away like she we being robbed. James shook his head, already attuned to his wife's sound effects. "Mal!" Alice scrambled from the booth and pulled her friend into a hug, careful of the baby. "Oh my gosh, oh my gosh," she stage-whispered. "Is this her?"

Beckett joined them, weighed down with the carrier and diaper bag. "No, it's a stunt baby we picked up for outings."

Alice pointed at him and laughed. "Nice try. I can see her puff of red hair from here."

At her friend's words, Mallory frowned. "I think it's getting darker every day." She peeled off Maybelle's tiny little beany, showing off a shock of strawberry blonde curls.

James stood, joining the group and leaning down to see little Maybelle. "She's cuter than I remember." He clapped Beckett on the shoulder. "Congratulations, she's a doll."

"Thanks, man." The tips of Beckett's ears turned red, but the loving smile he gave his wife and daughter could have melted the paint from the walls. The guy was a ball of love.

Before James could offer the other side of their booth to their friends, Alice shoved her coat and purse away and waved down Helen for a highchair. "Helen, we need you, please!"

The older woman came back with drinks for the young

parents and a highchair for Maybelle. "Get this out of your system, kid. Most people don't find you as charming as I do." She poked the baby in her belly and sauntered off, leaving Beckett to set up a place for his daughter.

"So, how have things been?" James asked, tugging Alice into the booth so Mallory could sit. Excitement radiated from the two women, as they tittered on about everything and nothing.

Beckett, as well accustomed to Mallory and Alice's hijinks, settled into his side of the booth and drank from his water before answering. "Short answer, fabulous. Slightly longer answer, exhausting, terrifying, and exciting."

James rubbed his chin. "I can only imagine."

Just as Beckett opened his mouth to say something, Maybelle spit up all over her blue snowflake onesie. "And this is why I packed four outfits for a two-hour sojourn."

Alice grimaced, pointing to Maybelle as she waved her tiny arms in the air. "Is that normal?"

Mallory scoffed. "This is actually light. You should have seen the mess she made at Ev and CeCe's place yesterday. They'll be washing puke out of that blanket until their own babies arrive."

James smiled sympathetically. "Sounds like we almost missed the Buckeye Falls Baby Boom," he quipped.

"I wouldn't say we missed it," Alice retorted, winking at her husband.

Despite their love for their nieces, nephews and friends' children, the only titles Alice and James were interested in were *aunt, uncle, artist, writer, husband, and wife.* The child-free discussion happened long before they got married, and Alice and James were happy with their choices. As much as their friends wanted children was as much as Alice and James wanted their careers and travel. Everyone was where they were supposed to be, and that was a comforting notion.

Twenty minutes later, their little fivesome munched on club sandwiches and Maybelle enjoyed her clean onesie that was covered in tiny reindeer. "Tell me about your show in

Toronto, James." Mallory shook a baby bottle like she was making martinis, deftly swapping Maybelle's pacifier for her lunch.

"You didn't even break eye contact," Alice remarked, pulling a piece of bacon free from her sandwich and eating the whole strip in one bite.

"Mal's a natural, not that I'm surprised." Beckett kissed her cheek, then turned back to James. "The show went well?"

James wiped his mouth with his napkin, resting his hand on Alice's knee. He squeezed it twice before answering. "It went really well. It was my first time doing a show with all statues, but it was a lot of fun."

Mallory whirled her arms in the air, making a corkscrew motion. "Were these the pieces you guys showed us last year in your house? The ones that looked all swirly."

James's face cracked into a megawatt grin that made him popular on social media. Even middle age didn't blunt his attractive face; something his agent and wife both loved. "Yes, the swirly ones. I still painted the wood once it was warped and set, but it was a departure from my normal paintings."

"Addy said it was one of James's most popular shows. He already has three requests for the new year." Alice beamed at her husband, clearly sharing his agent's enthusiasm.

When they'd gotten together, James was at a professional crossroads. He'd ended his first marriage, which was great for him personally and disastrous professionally. Alice had been his muse, inspiring him to create colorful paintings that sold faster than he could paint them. In their private moments, when he was in the studio working and she was curled up in her writing nook drafting ideas, James felt a peace like he'd never known before. Alice simultaneously made life chaotic and calm, and he'd never change a thing.

"How long are you in Buckeye Falls for this time?"

Mallory asked, snaking a hand out to snatch Beckett's last French fry.

Alice cocked her head, mentally scrolling through her calendar. "Through January, then it's off to Chicago for a book signing and then to New York so James can meet with some gallery owners."

Mallory laughed. "You guys keep getting busier and busier."

"Yeah, I don't know how you do it." Beckett agreed, handing his wife a napkin for Maybelle's latest spit-up. "We have a farm and a baby, and I can't even remember what day it is. Throw in jetlag, and I'd be all thumbs."

James nudged Alice and winked. "You get used to it. Fortunately, Alice is basically a human alarm clock."

Helen appeared with two to-go boxes and the check. "Here's a mixed box of Christmas cookies, courtesy of your sister-in-law," she said to Mallory. "And here's the check. I don't care who pays, but I'll take it up at the register." She backed away from the table after patting Maybelle on the head.

James snatched the ticket and tucked it in his shirt pocket. "Hey," Mallory protested. "We invaded your lunch, it's the least we can do."

"Save the money for a new outfit for Maybelle." Before Beckett or Mallory could thank him, Maybelle produced a sound that would make any fifth grader snort with laughter as she filled her diaper.

"Holy crap." Alice coughed into her fist. "Is she for real right now?"

Beckett's head fell back as he laughed, his red hair falling off his face. "This is nothing. You should come by after strained pears day."

Alice pinched her nose and shuddered. "Hard pass."

Mallory made to get up, but Beckett put a hand on her shoulder. "I'm up, you stay and relax."

"I won't argue with that," she said, pulling Beckett down for a quick peck before he disappeared into the restroom with Maybelle and her atomic diaper.

Sensing the girls wanted a few minutes alone, James pulled himself to standing and held up his cell. "I'm going to pay Helen and call Addy quick. She's been texting about one of the pieces from Toronto."

Alice mouthed *I love you* as he waved at Mallory.

Finally alone for a moment, the women leaned in and started giggling. "You guys seem really good," Alice said, relieved that motherhood hadn't changed one of her favorite couples.

Mallory flushed but nodded. "I was about to say the same thing about you and Mister Fancy Pants Artist. You're still loving the traveling?"

Alice nibbled her bottom lip while she pondered her answer. "Yes, we both love the traveling. But I'm only now realizing how much I've missed."

Mallory waved off her friend's concern. "Alice, you've only been gone three months, and we were so busy I couldn't have seen you as much as I wanted to anyway. Between getting the farm bakery ready and everything with Maybelle, it's been go, go, go."

"Okay, you've assuaged my guilt. Thanks, Mal." Alice reached across the table and took her friend's hands in hers. "She really is a gorgeous little doll."

Mallory shimmied in her seat and beamed. "She really is. She has my nose for sure, and her eyes are definitely like Ev's."

Alice giggled. "Clearly she inherited her father's hair. What a little carrot top."

Mallory rolled her eyes. "Yes, okay, fine. She has Beckett's hair. I wanted a little mini-me with boring brown hair, but I guess I'll have a little red-headed princess."

"Speaking for redheads everywhere, I'm offended." Beckett appeared at the table, a sleeping Maybelle resting on his shoulder. "I'm going to take her out to the car and settle her in. You ladies take your time."

"You're the best, Beckett. Don't listen to this person,"

Alice teased, kicking Mallory under the table.

"Love you both!" Mallory singsonged as Beckett left with the baby and the box of cookies he'd taken without his wife noticing.

"Any chance you're free for a little retail therapy this week? Not only do I need to do all my Christmas shopping, but I could stand for a new outfit."

Mallory clapped. "Yes, dear Lord, yes!"

"When is good?"

Pulling her phone from her purse, Mallory scrolled through her calendar. "Tomorrow my parents are taking Maybelle to have a grandkids day, so I'm free all afternoon."

"I'll meet you at Frick and Frack at noon," Alice said.

"It's a date."

Both women scooted out of the booth and hugged each other.

"It's so good seeing you, Alice. I've missed you."

"Missed you more," Alice agreed. While she wasn't short on friends, she didn't have any friends like Mallory. Keeping their girl time on the schedule was important to Alice, and she looked forward to playing catch-up with all she missed.

On their way out, Max waved from the counter. "See you ladies on Christmas!"

"Looking forward to it," Mallory said, as Alice quipped, "You couldn't keep us away."

Stepping out into the winter chill, Alice felt around for her scarf. "And I think I left everything in the car," she groaned, her forgetful nature still in tack.

Before Mallory could reply, both of their cars pulled up to the curb. James lowered the window, tossing a hat and scarf at his wife. "Here we are. Can't have you turning into a popsicle."

"You guys are still too freaking cute," Mallory said, pulling Alice in for one more hug. "See you tomorrow."

Beckett lowered the driver's side window and waved as Alice got into the car. James had already turned on the heated seats and was playing her favorite Christmas station.

"Ready to go home and write for a bit? Addy gave me some ideas for the next show, and I'm eager to get working."

Alice leaned across the car and kissed James, taking her time to savor the flavor of his cinnamon gum. "Take me home, husband."

"Anything for you, wife."

CHAPTER 5
Making a list, checking it twice

"You're sure you have enough food ordered?" Natalie asked from her desk, heels kicked off and feet resting on top of the filing cabinet.

Ginny lounged in the chair opposite; her own shoes long forgotten. She swirled a coffee mug filled with merlot; her eyes slightly unfocused. She hiccupped and recovered before answering her friend's question. "Have you met my husband? I don't know if you know this, but he's a chef who has run several restaurants for nearly twenty years. He knows how to order turkey and bread crumbs."

Natalie snorted. "You're right, I'll shut up about that." She reached out, toying with a sparkly pencil holder Otis made the previous year as a Mother's Day gift. The lumpy clay vessel was more reminiscent of a pile of dirt, but he'd thrown some glitter on to perfect the "girl touches," as he'd proudly shared his artistic abilities with her.

"You seem distracted," Ginny observed, flexing her toes and sighing after a long day. The holidays were wearing them all down in different ways.

"Sorry, just getting sentimental. I think it's Christmas— I usually get all goofy when we put up the tree."

Ginny cocked her head and laughed. "And what's your excuse for the rest of the year?"

Natalie rolled her eyes, twirling the pencil holder this way and that as she gathered her thoughts. "I think it's a lot of things. Anthony's new job, CeCe's about to become a mother, and Max is renovating the diner. It's all combined to put me in a pre-holiday funk." She made eye contact with her friend, and Ginny flushed, giving away her own distractions.

"Hey, lady, that's my line."

"You're worried about the diner renovations?" Natalie raised an eyebrow.

Ginny waved away Natalie's concerned expression. "No, I know Max has that all well in hand. Plus, the new place is going to be fantastic. He's put so much thought and care into it, it can't fail." She held up her hands, all fingers crossed. "But the diner is all of our place, you know?"

Natalie nodded sagely. "Oh, I know. I've had more good times in that old place than I can count." Natalie and Anthony had renewed their vows there, had shared countless family meals, and she and the girls had turned the diner into their own playground after hours. Natalie had lost track of how many nights were spent in the kitchen, with Ginny playing bartender while CeCe cooked up something delicious, Alice and Mallory rounding out their group with hilarious stories that had them clutching their sides. The diner was one of her favorite places, full stop.

Ginny hummed her agreement, lost in the musings of the past decade. When she'd moved back to town, before she'd reconciled with Max, the diner had been a thorn in her side. All the time Max spent within the walls of the restaurant used to make her resentful, but now it made her proud. He'd created a hive of activity that Buckeye Falls loved, whether you were new to town or a local with deep ties to the area.

"I think Christmas is the perfect send-off." Ginny nodded, rolling her bottom lip between her teeth to stop herself from crying. It could be the mid-day merlot break, or the fact that she had been distracted with the kids, but suddenly she couldn't believe all the change happening around her. She pulled her sleeves down, fingers fidgeting with the hems.

Natalie topped off their glasses and let out a breath. "We both have a lot going on, don't we?"

Ginny blinked and sipped from her wine. "Girl, that's an understatement." Squaring her shoulders, she got to the question she was dying to ask. "How are *you* holding up with the shift from First Lady of Buckeye Falls to First Lady of Ohio?"

Natalie scoffed, waving away the moniker. "First of all, I'm pretty sure that's the governor's wife. Secondly, I don't know."

For nearly fifteen years, Anthony had been at the helm of Buckeye Falls. Yet he wasn't the only Snyder with ties to town hall, as his father had been mayor for twenty years before Anthony. Buckeye Falls was about to enter a new era without a Snyder at city hall.

"It's a fair amount of change for the Snyder clan," Ginny surmised. "I don't think it's wrong that you're feeling a lot of things."

"I'm simultaneously thrilled at the change and petrified. Anthony will do amazing things, I know that in my bones, but we've gotten so settled in our routines, as hectic as they are, and it's wild to think of what's to come."

Ginny placed her cup on the desk and reached out, snaking Natalie's trembling hand in her own. "It's going to be amazing, you'll see. Anthony has done great things here, and it's only fair he spreads his wings and helps the rest of the Buckeyes out there." She winked and Natalie squeezed back with everything she had.

"Thanks, you're right. You'll never hear me argue that he's got the chops. It's just a little bittersweet that we're all moving on with things. I like our little nest."

Ginny nodded, reclining back in her seat. "Our nest isn't

so little," she said, jutting her chin toward the door. Even through the closed door, it was impossible to ignore the din of activity. What had started as two friends with a dream had turned into a small events empire. Staff had been hired and their book of business had tripled over the last five years alone. N&G had come a long way.

Just as Natalie opened her mouth to reply, their new assistant, Zoe, knocked on the door. Both women made a show of hiding the wine bottle, but it was no use. Their weekly wine meetings were common knowledge to not only the team at N&G, but most of Buckeye Falls. "Hiya," she said as she stepped into the office.

"What can we help with?" Ginny asked, turning around.

"Um, well. I know you're—she hesitated and looked at the nearly empty wine bottle—"in a meeting. But there's someone to see you. She doesn't have an appointment, and I asked her to—"

CeCe pressed into the office, nearly knocking poor Zoe on her butt. "Sorry," CeCe said as she pushed Ginny to the side and slid into the only other seat. "I tried to explain that I don't need an appointment, because I'm best friends with the owners. Plus, I needed to get off my feet."

Zoe glared as CeCe made herself comfortable, kicking her feet out to rest on the edge of Natalie's desk. Natalie saved the day by offering Zoe the next best thing to kicking CeCe out on the street. "Thanks, Zoe. Why don't you take the rest of the afternoon off? Our last appointment canceled, and you could probably use the time to wrap presents or do something festive." She flapped a manicured hand in the air, politely dismissing their newest hire.

"If you're sure?" Zoe asked, already backing out of the door.

"We're sure," Ginny confirmed, waving over her shoulder.

As soon as the office door snicked shut, CeCe rolled her eyes. "You two really hired some serious employees. Were they former Pinkerton Guards? Do you know I had to sweet talk my way back here for nearly two minutes?"

Natalie arched an eyebrow. "You know how to sweet talk?"

Ginny coughed and covered her smile with the merlot bottle. "I'll have you know I can be very sweet," CeCe protested. "When I'm not eight months pregnant with twins and hangry."

Natalie opened her top desk drawer and pulled out a bag of Halloween candy. She tossed it on the desk and gestured at the pile. "Please, help yourself, Momma. Every time I see you, you remind me why we stopped at two kids. Although, I do love squeezing the fluff out of little Maybelle." She sighed wistfully, popping another candy in her mouth.

Ginny snuck a piece herself. "What the babies want, the babies get." Through a mouthful of peanut butter she added, "and that mindset continues until they're out of high school."

CeCe didn't need to be told again, snatching up three mini caramel bars with lightning-fast reflexes. Biting into the first bar, she tossed her head back and made NSFW sounds. "God, why is chocolate so freaking good?"

Natalie unwrapped her own candy before asking, "What brings you in today? Other than free candy and a bathroom." Over the last three months, CeCe would use their office as a public restroom when nature called. At first it was entertaining, until a young intern stumbled in on CeCe having a moment that involved support hose that were stuck and the vocabulary of a longshoreman.

"I was in the neighborhood," CeCe said with a laugh. "Well, I wanted to check on the menu for Christmas. Between your husband"—she pointed an accusing finger at Ginny—"and mine, I can't get any answers on what's needed."

"Um, maybe they're keeping you in the dark since you're supposed to be on bed rest," Ginny shot back, smirking through her peanut butter cup.

Natalie frowned. "Yeah. Shouldn't you be at home on a

41

pile of pillows being worshipped?"

"I'm not a homebody. Have you two met me?"

CeCe was always on the go, and usually in a kitchen. If she wasn't in the diner, she'd be on their food truck or helping Max prepare for Max's Gin Joint. Not to mention, she'd been prepping menus for the bakery at Beckett's farm. She was used to being busy, and she hated feeling the lack of control that came with pregnancy.

"You're about to be the biggest homebody," Ginny said, holding up a finger and adding, "and that wasn't a fat joke. I'm actually impressed you're not bigger with the twins."

"The fact that you can still tie your own shoes is both impressive and really annoying," Natalie lamented, slurping from her wine. "When I was pregnant with Otis, I couldn't see my own ankles until he was out of diapers."

"I'll have you know I haven't seen my feet in ages. I manage the task by sonar. I'm like a bat." She squinted her eyes and flapped her arms, causing Natalie to choke on a Hershey's Kiss.

Ginny snorted, recovering quickly. "Going back to your Christmas question, Momma-to-be, it's covered."

Natalie nodded. "We were actually just discussing this when you interrupted our meeting."

CeCe scoffed, holding up the now empty bottle of merlot. "Oh yeah. I really interrupted a meeting of the minds."

"I only had a glass and a half," Ginny bragged.

"That's only because her husband isn't picking her up," Natalie retorted. "I'm getting a ride from Representative Snyder, so I can drink to my heart's delight." She punctuated her point by tossing back the last of her wine.

CeCe chuckled. "Why do I feel like you call Anthony that in the bedroom?"

"Do I want to know?" Anthony asked from the doorway. He was dressed in one of his navy tailored suits, his dark hair graying at the temples.

Natalie waved him over, leaning over the desk to smack

a kiss on his cheek. "Hello, Representative Snyder. We were just talking about you."

He turned to look at CeCe and Ginny before rolling his eyes. "Whatever she said, it's probably a lie."

"I asked if she—" CeCe's explanation was halted by Ginny's hand over her mouth.

"Ignore all of us. Happy hour started early, and we're glad you're here."

Anthony reached out and took a piece of candy from Natalie's desk, chewing thoughtfully while his wife tidied up their glasses and bottle. "Everything set for Christmas? Now that I'm no longer mayor, I actually have some time to help with cooking or whatever."

"No offense, JFK, but I want the professionals to handle the cooking," Natalie teased, striding over to her husband and adjusting his tie. "And is your replacement ready to take the oath?"

Anthony sighed but rallied quickly. "Yep. Mayor Josh is ready to go. Technically, he's in charge now until his official swearing in, but with the holidays, I'm hoping we can all relax."

Ginny collected the candy wrappers and laughed. "I can't believe Trudy's grandson won the election. And I really can't believe he won it on the platform of *Call me Josh*."

Making a show of rolling his eyes, Anthony helped Natalie into her coat, taking care to wrap her scarf around her neck. Trudy had been Anthony's assistant, and his father's before him, in town hall for decades. Apparently, her colorful stories about the job interested her twenty-five-year-old grandson to run for office. He'd worked in local politics a few towns over, and since no one was looking to fill Mayor Snyder's shoes, it was a runaway.

"Admit it," Natalie said when they were all bundled up. "You're going to miss the local political drama."

Anthony blinked, shoving his hands in his pockets. Three years before, he'd looked into running for state representative. It was a huge undertaking, and his campaign succeeded with the help of his detail-oriented wife. After the new year, he'd be sworn in as the newest state representative in Columbus. It was a job tailor-made for him, much like his navy suits.

"I might miss it a little," he lamented, helping CeCe to her feet. "And don't even say you're walking back to the diner. We're driving you home."

CeCe saluted and let Anthony hold the door for her. "I won't argue, but can you drop me at the Dairy Queen on the way out of town? We're craving some Blizzards." She enthusiastically rubbed her belly.

Natalie linked her arm through Anthony's and sighed. "That actually sounds really good."

Anthony jangled his keys like he was tempting a toddler. "All right, ladies. Follow me to the land of fat and carbs."

Ginny whined, "Oh, I want to go." She followed them outside into the crisp December air, locking up the flipping their sign to *Closed*.

Main Street was decked out in all its finery, with garlands hanging from storefronts, wreaths on the doors, the lamp posts wrapped in fairy lights. It was a scene from a *Hallmark* movie.

Striding ahead, Anthony opened the car doors for the ladies and waved to Ginny. "Tell Henry to break a leg tonight."

Natalie hopped in the passenger's seat and pointed at Ginny. "Yes, send him our best. I'll eat an extra ice-cream cone for you, since you're needed at Henry's pageant. And don't forget to send me the final Christmas menu."

"Like you'd let me forget." She checked her watch and winced. "And thanks for the reminder. I keep forgetting the show is tonight."

That wasn't true, she remembered. Max's concerns for their son's stutter had needled into her own thoughts, the stress weighing her down. In her heart, she knew Henry would rally. Just because his father struggled didn't mean Henry would follow precisely in his father's shoes. Henry loved the stage, and that passion should be enough to keep his words clear, whether he was singing or speaking. Or at least that's what she told herself…

The friends all waved goodbye before Anthony pulled onto Main Street. Fifteen minutes later, their SUV was filled with a dozen varieties of ice cream and a very contented CeCe. Ginny played Christmas carols at the highest volume her ears could handle, drowning out her fears as she crested the hill toward home.

CHAPTER 6
The voice of an angel

The community center was filled to bursting when Max and his family arrived. Mona had texted they saved them some seats up front, and Ginny found them quickly. Mona waved, the light catching the hundreds of sequins on her sweater. Around her neck was a set of Christmas lights that seemed to flash in morse code.

"Over here, guys." Harold stood and shuffled to the side for his granddaughter. "Hey, princess," he said, wrapping Josie in a bear hug.

To no one's surprise, Harold had taken his role of grandfather seriously before Josie was home from the hospital. He'd bought cigars with her initials and handed them out to everyone he knew in town, sometimes on several occasions. When Henry rounded out their family, he'd had ballcaps made with Henry's birthdate and wore it until the brim warped and the embroidery faded.

"Hi, Gramps." Josie hugged him back before leaning over and sharing the love with Mona.

Max and Ginny took their places, silencing their cell phones and shedding their coats. "Is our boy ready?" Mona asked as she handed everyone a program for the show.

"I think so," Ginny replied. "I heard him practicing his lines in his room before we left. He's really excited."

Beside her, Max tensed. His program was already rolled up tight, the paper creasing in his firm grip. Ginny covered his hands with hers and squeezed. "What if ..." Max whispered, careful to keep his voice low so Josie wouldn't hear.

"No what-ifs," Ginny chastised, pulling whatever confidence she had left. "Hen is ready, and he knows what he's doing."

Max leaned closer and added, "But he stammered in the yard the other day and ..."

Josie surprised her parents by scooting closer. She shook her head and looked older than her twelve years. "Henry is fine, guys. He was upset about Zippy, but you saw him today. He wouldn't shut the hell up."

Harold bit back a smile. "Language, princess."

"Sorry." She shrugged. "But I know I'm right."

Max pulled his daughter in for a hug, likely embarrassing her with the public display of affection. "Have I told you recently you're a great freaking kid?" He kissed the top of her head as tears threatened to fall.

"Pfft."

Their love fest was interrupted by the lights flashing. A stout man in a green sweater clambered up the stage and pulled the mic from its stand. "Good evening, everyone." The room quieted as he went over the program plans. "And as we get ready for the kids to wow us"—he paused to make jazz hands—"I remind everyone to silence their phones, avoid flash photography and ..." He hesitated before turning to Mona. "If you're wearing lights, we ask that you turn them off for the performance."

Mona winced, fumbling the power button on her necklace. Harold leaned in, and said, "I think you look lovely."

Ginny warmed at the display. Even after all these years, it filled her heart to see her father so happy. Her mother hadn't been in the picture for decades, and at first it seemed Harold was destined to roam the earth alone. Then Mona moved to Buckeye Falls and the rest was history. Ginny was sad they wouldn't be joining the festivities at Christmas, but Mona promised her son Tommy they would visit in Cleveland. Seeing as how she got to see them every week, Ginny knew she had to share.

"Without further ado, let the pageant begin!" The emcee clapped and hopped off the stage.

Both Max and Ginny had been at Henry's practices, so they knew he didn't come on until the third song. Everyone hummed along to the familiar tunes and clapped when the first soloist, a gangly girl the same year as Josie, finished her rendition of *Silent Night*. A pair of boys a few years younger than Henry then stumbled onto the stage. One of them played the recorder as the other sang the chorus of *Santa Claus is Coming to Town* six times before his mother began clapping to end the repetitive performance.

On their way off the stage, the shorter of the boys plugged his finger up his nose before flicking a booger on his friend. Josie made a gagging sound as Harold struggled to contain his laughter. "Boys are gross," she muttered, which earned a smug grin from Max.

"Sounds like we might have another few years before I need to buy a shotgun," he whispered in Ginny's ear.

She didn't have the heart to tell him she thought that time was closer than he realized.

Finally the time came for Henry's part of the show. He parted the actors on the stage, emerging with the confidence of a thirty-year-old Broadway star, not an eight-year-old novice. "And then the angels appeared ..." He threw his arms out theatrically, his voice as clear as a bell. The Sanchez clan watched in delight as Henry did his first scene with ease, never once stumbling or missing a line.

Max quaked beside his wife and daughter, holding back the tears until the end of the show. He was so proud of his son, proud of what he'd overcome at such a young age.

"He's killing it, Dad," Josie promised, leaning her head on his shoulder.

And he did kill it. Henry didn't miss a beat throughout the show. His monologues were funny, the timing on the songs perfect, and his voice never wavered—not once.

When the pageant ended, everyone in the community center erupted into cheers and applause. Josie stood on top of her chair, cupping her hands as she shouted, "You did it, Hen!" She added a few cat calls for good measure.

Ginny caught Max wiping his eyes with the back of his sleeve, and she couldn't keep her own tears at bay. Dabbing at her eyes with her sleeve, she took a deep breath and rallied for her son. While she knew he'd appreciate their emotions, she didn't want to cause a scene.

Harold was the first to greet Henry as he joined his family. "Henry, my boy." He eased down on his knees and nearly crushed his grandson's ribs with his enthusiasm. "That was the best show I've ever seen in my sixty-eight years."

"Thanks, Gramps," Henry said between squeezes.

Mona hip-checked Harold out of the way. "My turn." She giggled as she hugged Henry and peppered his face with kisses, leaving bright red lip prints in her wake. "Best performance I've seen. Oscar-worthy."

Henry pulled free and received a fist bump from Josie. He looked skeptical at his sister. "How was I?"

"Kicked ass, like I knew you would." She ruffled his black hair before stepping back and allowing their parents to envelop Henry.

"Hen," Ginny gushed as she hugged her son and husband.

Max rambled his praise until Henry got embarrassed and wiggled free. "Thanks," he said, straightening his sweater and wiping Mona's lipstick marks off his cheeks. "Can we eat now?"

"Yeah, buddy. We can eat now." Max draped his arm around Henry's shoulders and led the way to the exit. They had plans to go to the diner and celebrate with whatever Henry wanted—which would likely involve copious amounts of bacon.

As they approached the exit, Buckeye Falls' favorite troublemaker stepped forward. Mrs. Sanders stopped their exit, lifting her cane to block the door. Despite the festive occasion, she was dressed in black and looked ready for a funeral to break out. "Merry Christmas," she said, her greeting warm despite the *Lord of the Rings* routine.

Everyone smiled and returned the greeting. "What can we do for you, Mrs. Sanders?" Ginny asked, already fearing the answer. The woman was approximately three hundred years old, and she'd spent nearly all of those years stirring up trouble.

"It's supposed to snow on Christmas Eve." She said this with a hint of malice, like a witch in a children's fairy tale.

Max seemed undeterred. "Oh yeah?"

Mrs. Sanders swept a gnarled hand through the air. "Yes. Edna woke up with a kink in her neck this morning. Agnes said she hasn't felt her thumbs since Sunday night. I have swelling in my ankles, so we estimate the blizzard will arrive in time to muck up everyone's holiday plans."

Mona, never one to question the weather predictions of the elderly, covered her mouth with her hands. "Oh dear. We're supposed to drive up to Cleveland on Christmas Eve."

Mrs. Sanders frowned. "Might want to change your plans, Mona. You and Harold don't want to mess with that." She waved her other hand through the air, as if conjuring the snowflakes herself.

Harold, more pragmatic, tucked Mona against his side and smiled at Mrs. Sanders. "Thanks for the forecast, but I think we'll be all right. I haven't seen a word about this on the Weather Channel."

"The Weather Channel?" Mrs. Sanders threw her head back and barked. "Those hacks wouldn't know a hurricane if it blew up their asses."

Henry and Josie both snickered, earning a poke from Ginny. "Maybe Agnes should have those numb fingers looked at?" she suggested, sidestepping the older woman and creating an opening for her kids to escape.

"Pfft, that old girl is fine. When her digits get tingly, we know snow is coming."

"All the same," Ginny said with a frown.

Max shook Mrs. Sanders's hand and wished her a Merry Christmas for the third time before she finally stepped aside. Mona nibbled on her nails as they crossed the parking lot. "I'll check my phone in the car. If it's going to be bad, maybe we shouldn't go to Tommy's?"

Harold chuckled, still unconvinced that anything other than sunshine was headed their way. "I'm telling you, dear. It's going to be fine."

All talk of snow ended when they got to the diner. Evan was working that night, and he had a tower of bacon waiting on a plate for Henry when they arrived. "Here comes the man of the hour!"

CeCe wheeled out from the kitchen on Max's office chair. She was clad in her biggest chef's tunic, which strained under her belly. "Dude! I heard you slayed it." She clapped and whistled as they all poured into the corner booth.

Ginny pointed at CeCe's makeshift wheelchair. "Do I want to know?"

Max joined them, pulling off his coat with an eye roll directed at his favorite coworker. "You've got to be kidding me. This is hardly bed rest …or OSHA approved."

Evan rested his hands on his wife's shoulders and sighed. "This is the best I could do. I left her at home in a pillow fort with her favorite movie playing and a box of Lucky Charms. Twenty minutes later I get an Uber alert that my ride was here."

CeCe shrugged. "I couldn't sit there another minute, plus I'd already drank all the milk. You know I hate dry cereal. So, I thought I'd come see how the show went, and I knew you'd be pissed if I drove myself. Really, I was being responsible."

Ginny was incredulous. "So you took an Uber for a five-minute drive?"

"It's called compromising, Ginny." CeCe stuck her tongue out, earning a laugh from the group.

Helen joined the fray, doling out hot cocoa covered in whipped cream. Harold, Mona, and the kids nestled into the booth, eager for the celebration to continue. "Here you go, little man." Helen slid an oversized mug covered in marshmallows and chocolate shavings. "I hear you're the next Laurence Olivier."

"Who?" the boy asked, scrunching up his nose.

"Seriously?" Harold asked his grandson.

Mona *tsked*. "Next time you're over at our house, we're watching *Hamlet* or maybe *Wuthering Heights*."

"Good luck with that," Max said, joining his family. "If it's black and white, these two aren't giving it the time of day."

Josie nodded. "No offense, Gram, but this looks terrible." She scrolled through the actor's page on the IMDB app, scowling the longer she read.

Henry craned his neck to see, quickly agreeing with his sister. "Yeah, nope."

Helen snorted. "Sorry I brought it up."

Evan interrupted, pushing the plate of bacon toward Henry. "So other than a stack of bacon, what can I get everyone?"

Thirty minutes later, the table was covered in a variety of options. Evan and CeCe made everything family-style, piling platters and bowls with everyone's favorites. Max flipped the *Closed* sign a little early so they could take over the diner in peace.

"Aunt CeCe," Henry said from his spot in the booth. He'd inhaled two cheeseburgers and enough bacon to warrant a cholesterol statin. "Can I ride around on that thing when you're done?" He pointed to her vacated office chair.

"No," Max said as CeCe said, "Only if your dad isn't

watching."

Ginny, Mona, and Evan cleaned up while Harold pushed Henry and Josie back and forth in the office chair. Max loaded the dishwasher, closing the lid with a satisfying click. "All set."

Mona held her phone up triumphantly. "Look, the Weather Channel app says it'll be sunny on Christmas Eve."

Evan draped CeCe's coat over her shoulders before patting her belly gently. "Were they calling for snow?"

Max scoffed. "Mrs. Sanders and her crew are apparently blaming their aging bodies on the blizzard of the century."

CeCe frowned. "I'm glad it's not going to be bad. Evan's parents are traveling to Indiana to see his sister, and that would be a slog. We have enough on our minds without worrying about their travel."

Evan's eyes pinched, pulling CeCe closer to his frame. "I'm with CeCe—I hope this is nothing."

Harold took Mona's hand and stepped outside, bracing against the nighttime chill. "Do I need to remind everyone that the Weather Channel isn't calling for anything but blue skies on Christmas?" The only thing Harold watched more than the Cavaliers was the Weather Channel. No one was about to start an argument about the weather, especially with Harold.

Max held the door open as everyone else filed out into the cold December evening. Evan ran for his car so CeCe didn't have to walk. After getting her piled in and settled, they bid farewell and drove home, where he would likely duct tape his wife to the couch.

Ginny looked up at the sky, blinking at the chill. "I think it'll be fine," she said to herself.

"I know it will be, mostly because Agnes needs a doctor, not a meteorologist."

They hugged and kissed Harold and Mona before getting into their car with the kids. The sugar and excitement had worn off, with both kids falling asleep during the ten-minute drive home.

When he pulled the car into the garage, Ginny held her hand out to stop him from turning off the car. Bing Crosby crooned through the speakers, the only other sounds the kids' snores. "Tonight was perfect," she whispered, leaning in to kiss Max's cheek.

"It was," he agreed, turning his face so he could kiss Ginny on the lips. "At the risk of sounding corny, this might be the best Christmas ever."

Ginny smiled, her lips finding Max's once more. "It will be."

Pressing his forehead against Ginny's, Max said, "He was great. Not one hiccup."

"I knew he would be." Ginny sighed contently, relieved beyond words.

The moment was interrupted by loud barking from the house. Apparently, Zippy wanted to share in the family togetherness. Josie and Henry woke, unbuckled, and ran inside to play with the dog. "Don't even think about overfeeding him, Hen!" Max shouted as the door slammed shut.

"Merry Christmas, Max." Ginny wrapped her arms around his neck, pulling him close.

"Merry Christmas, Gin." Max turned off the lights, ushering his family to their corners for the night. As he unplugged the Christmas tree, he blinked back a fresh round of tears. Things were perfect; better than he could have imagined in his wildest dreams. Business was good, his family was healthy and happy, and it was his favorite time of year. He looked forward to sharing this feeling with his friends in a few days.

Max loved the residents of this quirky town, but he knew the snow wouldn't come. There weren't any white Christmases in their future this year; he was certain of that.

CHAPTER 7
Fa la la la la ... and all that jazz

"Alice! Addy's on the phone!" James called out from the studio.

James's agent and best friend, Addison, usually called him throughout the week as they prepped for shows. Yet when they were in between projects, their conversations dried up to the occasional text message. He didn't necessarily love losing touch with Addy during these creative periods, but they both understood the process. As soon as the paint dried on a new collection, they became inseparable yet again.

Their personal lives were also busier than usual. Alice was in the midst of her own creative process, with a book going through final edits and a proposal in the works for a new title. Addy was busy with work, but she and Chloe had finally moved in together after years of dating. She'd assured James that all was well in her romantic life, they were both just busy.

Alice sprinted into his workspace faster than a racehorse at the Kentucky Derby, her socked feet sliding across the polished cement, narrowly missing a stack of canvases. "Yeah, don't worry about those." He chuckled, moving aside a piece that would likely fetch a four-digit payday.

Completely undeterred, Alice held her hands out, and chanted, "Gimme, gimme, gimme," until he gave her the phone. "Hey, girl," she chirped. "Long time, no see."

Addison huffed a laugh, the sound of her heels echoing through the line. "Alice, it's been a week since I saw you."

"And that's too long," Alice said, pulling out one of James's work stools and making herself comfortable. He hastily moved a pile of pallets and brushes to the side before she accidentally elbowed them to the floor. "How's Chloe?"

Alice and James adored Addison's girlfriend, nearly as much as Addison did. She was sweet, funny, and kept their type-A friend fun and human. While Addison was an art agent constantly glued to her phone and always looking for the next big name in the art world, Chloe was reserved and worked for a non-profit in New York that focused on helping teens with tough home lives.

"She's fine. Still saving the world and making me proud. The stuff she deals with amazes me, yet she's always smiling."

"Chloe's a quiet powerhouse," Alice agreed.

"Right now she's not too happy with me, because we're still trying to figure out what we're doing for Christmas."

"Do I need to buy you a calendar?" Alice asked, unable to hide her judgment. "It's three days away."

"Thanks for the update, Julius Caesar." Addison's footfalls stopped, and Alice heard her mutter something before a series of beeps. "And I'm about to enter the subway, so you'll probably lose me. I just wanted to say hey. I miss you two already. Do you think you'll make it up to NYC after the holidays?"

"For sure. I need to confirm my book signings with the publisher, and James wanted to check in with one of the studios you mentioned."

Addison sighed dreamily. "If only I was also a literary agent. I'd get you and James all the best deals."

"He needs you more than I do. Tell Chloe we said hey,

and after Christmas, we'll figure out a time for you girls to visit. I miss our slumber parties."

Addison and Chloe had visited Buckeye Falls countless times over the years. At first, Addison bristled at the small-town and slower pace, but the more they visited the more she fell for Buckeye Falls' charms. Chloe was from a small town in Pennsylvania, so she relished the chance to slow down and smell the roses … and eat at the diner.

"We might take you up on that. I'm craving some of that midwestern home cooking."

James huffed as he walked past Alice. Leaning into the phone, he said, "You miss me cooking for you."

"God, I do love that kitchen. I keep threatening to move in while you guys are on the road."

Alice took the phone back, and said, "You have a standing invite. We love hosting you both."

"Yeah, yeah." Addison's voice garbled as she got lower into the subway station. "I'm about to lose you, so I'll let you go. Love you both. Merry Christmas!"

James and Alice said, "Merry Christmas, Addy!"

Alice disconnected and handed James his phone. "We really should get a time for them to visit on the calendar. It's great being back here, but I miss our city friends."

James tucked his phone in his pocket and nodded. Stepping near, he pulled Alice in for a hug. "Can you take a writing break? I was thinking of having a lazy afternoon. Just you, me, a pizza, and some cheesy Christmas movies."

Alice squealed, pulling James down for a kiss and running her fingers through his hair. His inky locks felt like silk in her hands, and she wiggled closer. "Maybe we can take a brief detour to the bedroom on the way to the couch?"

James dipped, wrapped his arms under Alice, and hauled her in the air. "Wife, that is the best idea you've ever had."

Just as they headed down the hall, a tangle of limbs, the doorbell rang. "Were you expecting anyone?" Alice asked between kisses, her hold still firm on James's collar. Their tenth wedding anniversary was on the horizon, yet she still felt like a newlywed.

"The only person I expected to see is in my arms." He winked, closing the distance for another kiss.

Alice swatted his chest and sighed. "Aww, babe. That's really sweet."

"I have my moments."

The doorbell rang again, this time followed by a series of knocks and a muffled "We know you're home. We see your cars."

"It's the kids," James said, disentangling his wife from his torso. "I didn't know they were coming." The smile he flashed Alice melted her heart. He loved those kids and enjoyed hosting them as much as she did.

Alice straightened her shirt and followed James to the door. By the time he unlocked the deadbolt, Otis had pushed his way inside. "Hey, Uncle James." James managed to snag a fist bump before the boy dove onto the couch, sending a pair of decorative pillows flying in the air. "You guys have lunch yet?"

Madeline followed her brother inside, carrying two tote bags and an eye roll. "Thanks for helping, O."

Otis grunted as he found the remote and turned the TV on. "I was thinking maybe pizza?"

Alice snorted and closed the door, following Madeline into the kitchen where James was already pulling out cans of pop for the kids. "Are you sure he's not my son? I'm pretty sure I did that routine with your parents."

"Maybe it's payback?" James teased, handing his wife a glass of wine. "Looks like I'll order two pizzas." He winked and headed to the living room. "Otis, you feeling pepperoni or sausage today?"

With the boys distracted with pizza toppings, Alice helped Maddie unload her bags. "What is all this?" she asked, holding up a bag of flour.

"Mom and Dad are busy with …" Madeline huffed as she tossed a bag of chocolate chips on the counter. "Stuff, and I wanted to bake cookies." She upturned the rest of the first bag on the counter, causing a bottle of vanilla extract to roll toward Alice.

Scooping up the bottle, Alice helped line up the baking supplies. Her niece was quiet, jaw tense as she carefully nudged a shaker of cinnamon in line. "You want to talk about it?" she asked, bumping Madeline gently in the ribs. "I happen to be a pro when it comes to family drama."

"It's not drama necessarily," she hedged, "but they're so busy getting Dad ready for his new job, plus all the holiday stuff." Madeline sighed, a lot more heavily than a girl that age should have to.

Alice's heart stopped. "Are things bad at home?"

Madeline shook her head so forcefully, her blonde ponytail hit her cheek. "No, nothing like that. It just doesn't quite feel like Christmas, you know? We haven't baked yet, and Grandma and Grandpa are still on their cruise." She reached out and snatched Alice's hand, squeezing it once before folding the tote bags into tidy squares. "I'm just glad you and Uncle James are back. I was starting to feel like Christmas wasn't going to feel as festive."

Alice pulled Madeline into a firm hug, kissing her temple. "Maddie, you're in luck. James and I were just about to watch a million Christmas movies and binge eat pizza. Let's start baking these cookies and have a full festive day."

Madeline beamed. "Really? You don't mind me and O barging into your day?"

"Not one bit." Alice pinched her cheek then turned toward the counter. There was a slim bag resting against Madeline's purse, and Alice reached for it assuming it was more baking supplies. Madeline stopped her with a trembling hand on her elbow.

"Wait! That's something else." Her cheeks flushed, and she yanked the bag from Alice's grip. "I uh, wanted to ask Uncle James about something."

James entered the kitchen with an empty can of pop and a concerned expression. "Is it normal for Otis to chug a pop in less than ten seconds?"

Madeline snorted. "I'm surprised it lasted that long."

Behind Madeline, Alice gestured to the bag and made a face. James raised an eyebrow but picked up on what she was trying to say with her manic expressions. *Ah, the perks of married life.*

Leaning on the counter, James poked at the mystery bag. "What's all this?"

Cheeks now turning radioactive, Madeline shrugged. "I thought, maybe if you have time, you could look at some of the pieces I've been working on for art class." She dipped her head lower, speaking directly to the countertop, and added, "I mentioned to one of my classmates that you're my uncle, and they thought you might be able to help with this."

James rubbed over his heart and nodded, swallowing twice before he spoke. "Maddie, I would love to take a look. We have at least an hour before those pizzas arrive. What do you say we head to the studio?"

"Really?"

James picked up the bag and gestured toward the rear of the house where his studio was. "Absolutely. Let's roll."

Madeline practically skipped after James, a spring in her step and a megawatt grin on her face.

Alice went to the fridge and pulled another two cans of pop for Otis. She took a moment to blink away a round of tears, her heart full at how much her husband loved her family … his family. "All right, buddy," she said as she tossed her nephew his sugar fix. "I'll be right back, then we're finding a Christmas movie that we both like."

Otis caught both cans, popping one open and downing the contents before Alice could walk away. *"Die Hard?"*

"Cue it up!" she shouted over her shoulder, heading toward the bedroom. As soon as she was inside, she pulled her phone out and called her sister-in-law.

Natalie answered right away, not bothering with pleasantries. "I'm hoping this call means my children are with you, as are the contents of our pantry."

Alice closed the door and flopped down on the bed. "Yep. Otis is drinking us out of house and home, and Maddie is showing James some of her art projects. We're going to bake cookies and watch holiday movies, if you don't mind."

Natalie sighed, but rallied quickly. "I don't mind at all. I'm sorry they left when we were busy. Anthony and I were working on wrapping their presents and checking on things at your parents' house while they're away. I promised Maddie we'd bake tonight, but I guess I wasn't fast enough."

"Everything okay with you guys?" Alice hated that she had to ask, that she couldn't stop herself.

"Yes, it's all been great. I think it's just that the reality of Anthony's new job, getting ready for Maddie's college applications next year, and Otis starting JV baseball in the spring, we just kind of imploded."

Alice groaned. "College applications already? I'm still getting used to Maddie driving."

"Girl," Natalie said with a cackle. "You should see your brother. Anthony is hardly handling it well."

"I can only imagine." Her brother was utterly devoted to his family, and she knew he had the biggest soft spot for his little girl. Thinking of Madeline's sullen mood, Natalie threw an idea at Natalie. "What are you and Anthony doing later today?"

"We were going to bake with the kids."

Alice sat up, giddy with her idea. "You're still going to, but I have an idea."

Natalie laughed. "Oh boy, I'm all ears."

"Give us a few hours with the kids. We ordered pizza for lunch, but eventually they'll tire of food and TV. You and Anthony enjoy the afternoon to yourselves, but join us for baking. Maddie seemed a little down that my parents aren't around, and maybe a little forced Snyder bonding will change her tune."

"That's a great idea. How about we swing by around six? I was going to make chili, so I can bring that with me."

Alice beamed, already hungry for her sister-in-law's famous chili. "Perfect. See you then."

*

"Good news, honey!" Natalie shouted into the living room, sliding her cell phone back into her jeans pocket. "The kids are alive and with your sister."

Anthony strode into the kitchen, a cluster of tape stuck to the front of his sweater. He'd been on gift-wrapping duty for the last hour, and apparently he was over it. "I figured they hadn't run off to join the circus," he said, rubbing his lower back with a groan. "I think I'm getting too old. I shouldn't have back pain from wrapping a video game."

Natalie approached her husband, carefully peeling the tape ball from his clothes. "You should have used the kitchen counter. There're hardly any secrets with the kids and their gifts." Natalie rolled her eyes. Both kids had shared their Amazon wish lists back in August, as they were very particular. The days of surprises under the Christmas tree were sadly over, replaced with electronics, cosmetics, and other grown-up requests. Both parents were eager to spoil their children, but Natalie would be lying if she didn't admit to missing the doll babies and dinosaur toys.

"So what's the plan for the rest of the day?" Anthony kissed her quickly before rummaging in the junk drawer for the ibuprofen. "I thought we were going to do holiday stuff once I was done with my notes for work." He threw two pills in his mouth and swallowed them dry.

"That's still the plan, but we're changing the location. We're going over tonight after I make a pot of chili."

Tossing his head back, Anthony made an NSFW sound. "I cannot wait. You haven't made that in a minute." Natalie's chili was famous in town for its spice and the array of toppings Natalie always included. If you didn't leave with heartburn and covered in corn chip crumbs, you weren't living.

"I just need an hour to get everything prepped." Turning to the cabinet, she retrieved a few cans of beans, but Anthony stopped her progress with a hand to her shoulder. She spun to face him, a tower of pinto beans between them. "What is it?"

"Thank you," he muttered, staring into her eyes. His were flinty storm clouds, and Natalie frowned.

"For what?"

Resting his forehead on hers, Anthony sighed. "Getting me elected. I know the last two years haven't been a picnic, but I couldn't have done it without you, Nat. And now you've got Christmas well in hand; you continue to impress me. I love you."

Natalie's bottom lip trembled while she tossed the cans with a clatter onto the counter. "Oh, honey, I love you, too." She wrapped her arms around him, running her fingers through his hair. "It was my pleasure to help, because I know you're going to be the best state representative Ohio has ever seen."

Anthony's cheeks turned pink at her praise. He dipped his head to capture her lips in a passionate kiss, filled with years of love, promise, and devotion. In his haste to get closer, he knocked another can onto the floor. It rolled all the way across the kitchen until it hit the fridge. "I need those for dinner," she said in between kisses.

"And you need an hour for the chili?" he asked, nibbling her ear lobe.

"Uh-huh?" Natalie asked, her brain currently focused outside her recipe book.

Anthony pulled back and made a show of checking his watch. "And we're not expected until dinner?"

Natalie raised an eyebrow. "I know that look." Waggling his eyebrows, he kissed her again. He whispered something in her ear, causing the hair on her neck to rise. "Representative Snyder, I'm scandalized," she teased, trailing a finger along his jawline. His five o'clock shadow had turned white over the election, but she loved it. Her husband was aging like her favorite bottle of merlot.

"Don't tell the voters," he said with a wink, leading the way to the bedroom. Natalie nearly stumbled in her haste to make it upstairs, grinning like the lovesick fool she was.

*

Five hours, two pizzas, one movie, and four gallons of soda later, Natalie and Anthony barged through the front door. Anthony carried a stock pot large enough for Otis to hide inside, Natalie behind him with a box. "Ho, ho, ho, we're here!" she said, kicking the door shut.

James hurried to help Anthony with the pot, while Alice relieved Natalie of her load. "What's all this?"

"Cheese, sour cream, corn chips, and a million other toppings for the chili. I couldn't remember what everyone liked, so I went a little overboard."

As soon as the first bowl clattered onto the counter, the kids arrived with ravenous expressions. "Please say that's dinner, I'm starving." Otis pushed his way to the front of the line, nearly trampling his sister and aunt's feet in the process.

"Wow, it's a shame you didn't just finish a whole pizza," Alice remarked, still shocked her nephew didn't weigh a metric ton.

James ruffled Otis's hair as he served his chili, adding a worrisome amount of corn chips to the bowl. "I was impressed with his restraint. When he realized his aunt didn't get anything, he gave you that corner piece."

Alice fluttered her hand in front of her face. "It was a gift I will cherish."

Otis rolled his eyes before strolling back to the living room. Madeline made up her dinner and followed her brother to the peace of the couch.

"Now that we're alone," Anthony deadpanned, doling out bowls for the adults. "How are you guys settling back in?"

The foursome fell into the easy conversation they'd perfected over the last decade—the men laughing about something at town council, the women gossiping about the kids and their friends. It was comfortable and warm, like that ugly holiday sweater you pull out after Thanksgiving.

"I think it's time for cookies," Natalie suggested as she helped herself to a second glass of wine. "Are we making traditional Snyder chocolate chip and those lovely little honey cookies James makes? What are they called again?"

James helped Anthony clear their dinner dishes, answering, "Yakgwa. I have the ginger syrup ready in the fridge."

"Did I hear the magic word?" Madeline asked as she joined them in the kitchen. "I was telling Josie about those last week. I love yakgwa."

Otis, the far less adventurous eater in the family, came in and helped himself to another pop. "We're doing chocolate chip though, right?"

Anthony tossed an apron to his son and smiled. "We're doing it all, O." Otis returned his father's matching grin and tied the apron.

The six of them rolled, shaped, baked, and fried cookies for hours, taking breaks to sample their work and nibble on leftover corn chips.

"This is magic." Madeline hummed as she scraped a blob of cookie dough free from a wooden spoon. "Just what I wanted."

Natalie looped an arm around her waist, nuzzling closer for a kiss. "I'm glad, Maddie. We need to do more things like this. Don't let me forget."

"I won't." She surprised her mother by returning the kiss and then loaded the dishwasher.

After everything was baked, the dishes clean and put away, the six of them staged an Instagram-worthy selfie. "Send it to Mom, please?" Anthony asked as he licked honey syrup from his thumb.

"On it," Alice announced as she shared the photo in a

group text chain.

Less than a minute later, their parents replied with *Oh, what fun! Wish we were there instead.*

Anthony huffed out a laugh when he read the text. "Oh yeah, because a cruise around the Greek islands is torture."

"I think next year we should go on a cruise for Christmas," Otis said, polishing off his fifth cookie of the night.

Anthony muttered something about the cost, but Natalie swatted him away with a tea towel. "I think that's worth looking into, O."

Otis turned to his aunt and uncle, and said, "That's parent speak for 'not going to happen.'"

"She didn't say that," Anthony replied, trying to stifle a grin.

Madeline yawned and Otis rubbed his eyes, tell-tale signs they were ready to crash from the sugar and general excitement of the day. "We'll see you guys at the diner for Christmas, right?" Madeline asked.

"Absolutely. I'll be ready with some notes on your painting by then." James shot a thumbs-up and Madeline shrugged.

"I mean, whenever."

"And I mean by Christmas." James slung an arm around her shoulder as they walked to the door. "You're a talented artist, Maddie. Don't start doubting yourself now."

She flushed the color of cranberries before hugging James and Alice and tugging Otis free of the cookie bowl. "You can't eat in my car. I just had it cleaned."

"Then I'm riding with Mom and Dad," Otis grumbled, snatching another cookie for the road.

James closed the door once everyone was gone, joining Alice on the couch with one of their favorite blankets. The lights were low, only the Christmas tree lighting the space. It was warm, cozy, and intimate—just how Alice liked it.

"I know I keep saying this," she murmured, "but I love that you love my family."

"Of course, what's not to love?" He pulled her closer, resting his chin on her head.

Alice leaned in, savoring the warmth of his touch. "You think Maddie has talent?" She nibbled her lip, fearful of the answer. She knew James would play it up if their niece wasn't any good, but it pained her to think she was terrible.

"She seriously has some chops. In fact, she reminds me a lot of myself at that age. Hungry to paint, but afraid of the results. I think with a little confidence, she'll find her way."

"Good thing she has a famous artist as an uncle."

James snorted. "I'm sure that won't hurt either. Maybe Addy can get her a show."

"I don't doubt it."

They sat on the sofa, wrapped up in each other until they fell asleep. James woke first, carefully carrying Alice to the bedroom and tucking her in beside him. As his eyes closed, he thanked his lucky stars for the millionth time that fate had brought Alice, and the crazy Snyder clan, into his life.

LIBBY KAY

CHAPTER 8
The Eleventh Hour

"That's the last of them," Beckett said with a sigh. He leaned back at the kitchen table, studying the stack of Christmas cards that were finally ready to mail. "I think they'll only be a week late at this rate."

Mallory groaned, swapping Maybelle to her other arm. "At least they should arrive before the New Year. And can people really blame us? We had a baby, for Pete's sake." She jostled the child in question, earning a giggle from the tiny redhead.

Beckett stood, collected the stack, and put them in a box. He leaned down and kissed both his girls on the forehead. "I'm going to go to the post office and mail these, otherwise we might as well wait for Maybelle's graduation announcements."

"Perish the thought. I'd never hear the end of it." Mallory followed Beckett to the door, holding out his hat with her free hand. "Do you mind picking up the stuff to make your famous apple crisp? I know Max said all the food is covered, but I hate not bringing something."

"You got it," Beckett agreed, opening the door to a whoosh of cold December air. "Gosh, this feels like snow

71

weather." He sniffed the air and exhaled slowly. "Smells like it, too."

Mallory giggled. "How can you tell?"

Beckett looked up to the gray sky and smiled. "Gram always said you could smell the snow, because the air is a little sweeter, a little heavier. She threatened to bottle the scent if she could, saying it would be more popular than our apple candles."

Maybelle sneezed at the cold air, earning coos and kisses from her parents. "Enough snow talk," Beckett said. "I better get going so I'm back in time for dinner. What time are Evan and CeCe coming over?"

"Five, but I wouldn't be surprised if they're early for a little Maybelle time."

"Then I better hurry." Beckett flashed her another smile, making Mallory weak in the knees. "Love you, Mal." Kissing the top of his daughter's head, he added, "Love you, too, little Belle."

Mallory closed the door and settled the baby into her pack and play. "Please behave for Mommy for two seconds, okay?" Maybelle cocked her head and coughed, a sweet little sound that made Mallory sigh. "And you better not be getting another cold. We can't get Auntie CeCe sick."

Taking the moment alone, she got Maybelle set up with some toys and turned on *White Christmas* for company. Beckett would be home before she knew it, and his gifts wouldn't wrap themselves. Just as Mallory taped the last corner of wrapping paper on a new pair of work boots, the front door flew open.

Knowing Beckett would never make such an entrance, she scooped up Maybelle and shouted, "In here, Ev!"

Evan and CeCe shuffled into the living room, Evan's hand pressed to CeCe's lower back. "Have a seat, babe. Right here," he said, not stepping back until she was on the couch.

CeCe rolled her eyes and kicked her feet, now unable to reach the ground. "I know where the couch is, Ev. Please save the babying for a month from now when the kiddos come." Evan gritted his teeth, stifling a retort, as he fluffed pillows and rested them behind his wife. He shook open a blanket and draped it over her legs before stepping back and thrusting his hands on his hips, nodding when he felt she was protected.

Mallory snorted. "No offense, but I'm loving this a little too much."

Evan playfully shoved his sister on the way to the kitchen. "Where's Foxy? I need an ally."

"Running errands in town. We are woefully late on the Christmas cards."

"Pfft, no one cares about that. You have a baby, doesn't that mean you're allowed to be late with everything for at least a year?" CeCe reached out for her niece, wiggling her fingers until Mallory handed her over.

Mallory joined her brother at the fridge. "CeCe, we have orange juice. You want some?"

"Yes, please. And anything with cheese. I'm starving."

Evan pulled out the bottle of juice and a wedge of cheddar, tucking them in his arm as he helped himself to a beer. "She's acting like we didn't stop for burgers on the way here. I just watched her inhale a cheeseburger faster than it took me to buckle my seat belt."

Mallory chuckled, pulling out a sleeve of crackers, a chunk of gouda, and a bunch of grapes to make an impromptu cheese board. "It'll calm down soon enough," she promised before quickly amending, "the eating part, I mean."

Evan patted his growing belly and sighed. "I hope so, Mal. At this rate, I'll weigh three hundred pounds by the time the twins arrive."

Mallory flicked her brother's stomach, which admittedly had grown throughout his wife's pregnancy. "You know you don't need to eat every time CeCe does, right?"

"Ha! And risk her thinking she's fat and has a problem?" He lowered his voice and scoffed, "I expected more from you, Mal."

Saving herself from another round of scolding, Mallory carried the cheese tray into the living room. CeCe had turned the volume up on *White Christmas*. Both she and Maybelle watched a dance routine with wistful expressions. "God, this movie is so good."

"Isn't it?" Mallory agreed, plopping down next to CeCe and swapping the baby for a plate of food.

"Speaking of white Christmases," Evan said through a mouthful of gouda, "Mrs. Sanders is telling all of Buckeye Falls that we're getting a blizzard tomorrow."

"Really?"

Evan shrugged and handed a stack of cheese slices to CeCe. "So the old bag said."

"Don't let Mrs. Sanders hear you call her that. I'm pretty sure she could whoop your butt in her eighties."

"I'm not afraid of her," Evan pressed, although no one missed how he nibbled his bottom lip.

"Who aren't we afraid of?" Beckett asked, stepping inside and bringing a whoosh of cold air with him. He shook a few rogue snowflakes from his red hair, his hat forgotten in the car.

"Is it snowing?" Mallory asked, closing the distance to Beckett and helping him with his coat.

"Told you," Evan and Beckett said in unison.

Evan raised an eyebrow. "Mrs. Sanders got to you, too?"

Beckett shook his head. "No, Lawless. Gram passed down her sniffer." He tapped the side of his nose, knocking his glass askew. "I'll never miss a snowstorm with this thing."

"You're all insane, and I'm starving," CeCe announced from her perch. She kicked out her feet and groaned. "And I need a forklift, please."

Mallory held up her hand. "Beckett and I are on dinner duty."

"Then I guess that means I'm doing the *not-so*-heavy lifting." Evan winked, easing CeCe back to her feet and pressing a kiss to her cheek.

"Good save, babe," she quipped, shuffling down the hallway toward the bathroom.

A few minutes later, everyone was seated at the kitchen table sharing a pot of soup. "This is amazing," CeCe drawled, wiping down her bowl with a crust of sourdough."

"Coming from you, CeCe, I take that as high praise. It's one of Gram's old recipes. Sometimes when I'm feeling sentimental, I'll whip up a pot."

Evan rested his elbows on the table, his expression wistful. "Do you remember when she'd make this noodle soup and those grilled cheese sandwiches?"

"And Gramps would come find us in the orchard and make us come home to eat before everything cooled?" Beckett replied, his eyes shining through his smudged glasses. He was proud of himself, not bursting into tears at the memories. Despite the decade-plus that had passed since their deaths, Beckett still mourned his grandparents. Save for the Lawsons, they were his only family.

"I remember you guys were mad at me for weeks when I ate the extra sandwich, because you were too slow coming down the hill." Mallory grinned, enjoying the trip down memory lane. "In my defense, I waited patiently for you two knuckleheads to come in, but I wouldn't resist the siren song of cheese and bread."

Beckett snaked his arm around Mallory's shoulder, bringing her to his side. "Those were some of my favorite times."

Beckett, Evan, and Mallory had grown up together. While Evan and Beckett were friends, it was Mallory and Beckett who had formed a tighter bond that grew into love. It may have taken a little longer to find their own happily ever after, but it was worth the wait.

"So, I'm dying to know," CeCe said, changing the subject as she adjusted her seat.

Mallory didn't miss the wince when CeCe leaned back, and she reached out a steadying hand. "Do you need anything?" she asked, unable to avoid nurse mode.

Evan sensed the strain in her voice and knelt down beside CeCe. "Babe?"

CeCe threw her arms in the air and groaned. "For crying out loud, I'm fine. I'm just very pregnant and hungry."

Evan frowned. "But you ate three meals since lunch. I didn't even get a full bowl of soup."

That comment earned him a glare from CeCe and a flick to the forehead from Mallory. "Nice, Ev. Want to rub any more salt in the wound?"

"I. Am. Fine," CeCe repeated. "What I wanted to know was if Beckett was making his famous apple crisp for Christmas?"

Beckett shot a thumbs-up. "Just picked up the ingredients. Fortunately, we have a million apples in cold storage, so I've got it covered." He reached out to wipe a smudge of strained carrots from Maybelle's chin before adding, "And I hope you're making cheesy bites, if you can."

CeCe smirked. "I can, and I did. They're in the fridge at the diner. I only need to slice and bake."

Evan checked the time and frowned. "We should probably head out. There's still a lot to do before the big day."

Everyone shared their goodbyes and helped Evan and CeCe to their car. The snow flurries had stopped, but Beckett wasn't convinced that was the end of the snowstorm. "It's going to be a white Christmas, Mal. I can feel it."

"The perfect first Christmas for Maybelle." She sighed and leaned into his side. Beckett kissed the top of her head and enjoyed the moment of peace. He loved hosting their friends and family at the farm, and he thanked his lucky stars he didn't sell it when he had the chance.

This was home. This was his family's home, and he knew his grandparents would love to know that Mallory and Maybelle would make a whole new slew of memories on the farm. Life was good, and Beckett was a lucky man.

CHAPTER 9
Visitors of Christmas Present

"It's snowing," Ginny said, jaw on the floor at the kitchen window. "I can't believe Mrs. Sanders was right." She turned off the faucet, hung the damp wash rag on the sink, and pulled out the canister of dog food.

Zippy, recovered from his paw and stomach woes, was ready to eat. His legs tippy-tapped across the floor as Ginny scooped his kibble. When the bowl was full, she slid it over to the hound, chuckling when he didn't dive right in. "Sorry, bud. We're back to normal portions." Zippy cocked his head, sniffed, then tucked into his breakfast.

Henry and Josie shuffled into the kitchen, matching sleepy expressions. "Merry Christmas," Josie said as she poured two glasses of orange juice.

"Merry Christmas, you two." Ginny hugged her children, savoring the closeness for a moment before pulling back.

Not much of a morning person, Henry flopped onto a stool and rubbed his eyes. "Merry Christmas."

Giving a glass to her brother, Josie leaned against the counter. Her gaze snagged on the window, and she gasped. "It's snowing. Mom, did you see?"

Ginny was caught off guard by her daughter's childlike wonder. "I did. Isn't that wild?"

Henry slurped from his juice, his gap-tooth grin on full display. "Old Mrs. Sanders was right."

"Hen!" Ginny admonished. "We don't call her *old* Mrs. Sanders."

Henry slid his sister some side-eye, seeking confirmation. Before she could reply, Max entered the kitchen. He was dressed in his favorite cooking clothes: a worn flannel and jeans. "Merry Christmas you guys." He hugged the kids before planting a kiss on Ginny's lips. When he looked out the window, he inhaled. "Old Mrs. Sanders was right. Look at it go!"

"Max," Ginny said, poking him in the side with her coffee spoon.

Henry and Josie doubled over in fits of giggles. "I told you." Henry gasped in between peals of laughter.

Max raised an eyebrow. "What did I miss?"

Ginny shook her head, intent on keeping the peace and what was left of her sanity. "Nothing. Let's get coffee going so we can do presents."

At the mention of gifts, both children hopped off their stools and bounded into the living room. Max opened the fridge, pulled out a tray of unbaked cinnamon rolls and an egg casserole he made the night before. "We will have breakfast in an hour," he announced to the nearly empty kitchen.

Zippy sat on his haunches, waiting for a morsel to fall to the ground. When Ginny wasn't looking, Max peeled a piece of sausage from the top of the pan and tossed it to the floor. Zippy scarfed it down before Ginny was done adding sugar to her coffee.

"Don't open anything until we get there," Ginny warned, handing Max his coffee. "Those two will be done before you even get breakfast in the oven." She took a step to join the kids, but Max snaked his arm around her waist and pulled her close.

"Merry Christmas, Gin." He kissed her, slowly and with all the feeling called for on Christmas morning. Ginny's coffee mug was hastily slid across the counter so she could return her husband's passionate embrace.

"Merry Christmas, Max." Ginny rested her forehead on his chest, sniffing in the scent of worn cotton and Max. "I love you," she whispered, leaning into his hold.

He cupped her to him, breathing quietly and watching the snow fall outside. Despite the fact they'd been remarried for well over a decade, he never stopped to marvel at how lucky he was. During the darkest days of their divorce, he'd lain awake at night dreaming of this moment. A warm house, Ginny in his arms, two happy kids under the Christmas tree, and a goofy mutt running around for scraps. It was heaven; it was his life, and he would never take it for granted.

"Are you two done having a moment? Hen started shaking his presents, and I'm starving to death." Josie thrust her hands on her hips, looking closer to eighteen than twelve.

Ginny reluctantly stepped back, winking at Max before addressing their daughter. "All right, you win. Let's start the festivities."

Josie grinned and bolted back toward the Christmas tree, this time with Zippy on her tail.

Two hours later, and the Sanchez family Christmas was officially in the books. The kids were surrounded by wrapping paper piles and more gifts than they'd be able to use in a year. Ginny was thrilled with her new necklace from Max, and he was in love with the high-end knife set she bought him for his new restaurant. Henry was already playing with his new video game before they were done packing up for the diner.

"What time should we leave?" Ginny asked, hooking her new necklace into place and sighing at the sparkle in her reflection. It was a simple gold chain, with three gemstones hanging from the middle—one stone for each of the kids and Max's birth months.

"Whenever we're all ready. Evan just texted that he and CeCe are already there. Apparently bed rest was just a recommendation from her OBGYN." He did air quotes and scoffed. Everyone knew CeCe was unstoppable.

Ginny huffed. "I'm sorry, have you met CeCe? I'm surprised Evan hasn't tried chaining her to the bed."

"That's a visual I don't need." Max shuddered. "I'll give the kids a countdown and throw the rest of the food in the car. Ready in five?"

Ginny nodded before texting CeCe, Natalie, Mallory, and Alice that they were en route to the diner. She smiled as she tucked her phone into her purse and stepped out into their white Christmas.

Fat snowflakes fell around them, covering the yard in a blanket of white. Max had already warmed up the car, with the kids buckled in and playing with their new gadgets. Ginny checked that Zippy was inside before locking up and walking straight into the last person she expected to see.

"Dad?" she asked, stumbling in her snow boots. "What are you doing here?"

Harold steadied his daughter, offering her a sheepish grin. "Well, Ginnybread. Remember Mrs. Sanders' premonition?"

From down the driveway, Ginny saw Mona trudging up the sidewalk. Even through her scarf and open coat, Ginny could see her sparkling sweater. A pair of jingle bell earrings kept time with each step. Max spotted his in-laws and hopped out of the car. "Harold? Mona?"

"Merry Christmas!" Mona said, waving as she slid on a patch of ice. Max and Harold both rushed to catch her as she glided into one of the shrubs. "Ooh." She exhaled as she gained her footing.

"I guess Mrs. Sanders was right," Max mused as he ushered everyone to the car. "We've got room for two more, hop in."

Harold and Mona exchanged a look before stepping

inside. The kids waved from the warmth of the SUV, clearly excited to see their grandparents. "Hop in," Ginny urged, wrapping her arms around her middle.

"Are you sure there's room?" Mona asked, worrying her bottom lip.

Harold joined in the line of questioning. "I know this was meant to be your holiday with friends."

"Pfft, like we're going to leave out you two. Get in. The more the merrier." Ginny held the door open for Mona, instructing the kids to slide into the back row.

"You're sure, Ginnybread?" Harold asked, his brow furrowed. "You'll have enough food and space?"

Max wasn't having it. "You realize that CeCe and Evan have probably already cooked enough for an army, and we're hosting at the diner. Which is in a restaurant, which is closed to the public today. There is more than enough of everything to go around."

That offer was tested ten minutes later as they arrived at the diner. Standing out in the snow, having an animated discussion, was the entire Snyder clan. Alice flapped her arms in the air and shouted, "Will you please get inside? This is ridiculous."

"I will not be manhandled, young lady," her mother admonished.

James pinched the bridge of his nose, looking to Anthony for help. Unfortunately, the new state representative was busy negotiating with his father. "Dad, will you please listen to me and Alice? We have room."

Natalie stalked up the front door and held it open, gesturing wildly. "Can everyone please trust that there's room? I'm so cold my fingers are frozen."

Max strode up to the motley crew, pausing to wish the kids a merry Christmas. "Merry Christmas, guys." He fist-bumped Otis and patted Madeline on the shoulder. Otis went off to discuss Christmas gifts with Henry, leaving his sister to bicker with her grandmother.

Madeline was basically Natalie's twin, her blonde hair

almost as white as the snow and her eyebrow arched halfway up her forehead. Her hip was cocked as she tugged on her grandmother's sleeve. "Please, can we all go inside?"

Max wanted to help, but also get everyone out of the cold. "What's going on, Snyders?" turning to James, he added, "and Gibsons."

James offered a warm smile. "Donna and Steven decided to cut their Mediterranean cruise short to spend the holidays with family."

"Until we remembered our family had other plans," Steven helpfully added. The elder former mayor seemed less than thrilled with crashing his children's Christmas plans.

"We really can just go back to the house and wait until you're done celebrating." Donna wrung her hands together, glancing between James and Max. "I think that would be easier."

Ginny and her family joined the fun, ushering her and Natalie's kids inside. "I think we can all agree we'll have plenty of food and space. It's also Christmas, and no one is going to sit at home alone."

Natalie hitched a thumb at Ginny. "I'd do as she says. She can get tough when she wants to."

Everyone shared an awkward laugh as they filed inside the diner. Evan had turned on all the twinkle lights, casting the restaurant in a cozy glow. Tinsel, garlands, and various decorations hung from the ceiling and walls, bordering on tacky yet giving the desired effect. A playlist of classic Christmas songs played through the speakers, adding to the ambiance.

"You see, we were going to go to Cleveland to see my Tommy," Mona started, sliding into a booth with Donna, Steven, and Harold. "Then this snow kept falling, and now we're stuck." She flapped her hands, causing the jingle bell bracelets to clatter.

"Well, at least there's room for us," Donna added, anxiously looking over for reassurance as she toyed with her fair more tasteful diamond bracelet. These women were on opposite sides of Buckeye Falls' fashion spectrum.

Alice overhead and walked over to their table. "If you four don't calm down and enjoy yourselves, I'm going to tell Anthony. I'm pretty sure he has the authority to throw you in Grinch jail or something."

Otis overheard and got excited. "Holy crap, is that true, Dad?"

Anthony rolled his eyes. "Thanks for that, Alice. Now my son is going to threaten imprisonment to all his enemies."

"How many enemies can O have?" Alice asked, punching her nephew lightly on the shoulder. "This kid's a saint."

Steven coughed into his handkerchief, clearly unbelieving. "He's a good boy, but a saint?" He directed his question to his wife, who merely shook her head and took off her gloves.

"I'm going to go see if they need help in the kitchen," Alice suggested, catching Anthony's eye so he'd follow her.

As soon as they crossed into the kitchen, the Snyder siblings found CeCe and Max and began their long-winded apologies. "I'm so sorry about them," Alice said as Anthony nudged her to the side, and added, "They sprung this invasion on us this morning without a hint of notice. We were loading up the car, and boom, there they were like specters of Christmas past."

Ginny smiled, pausing her vegetable chopping to chime in. "I think it's sweet, they wanted to surprise you kids."

"Our parents don't believe in surprises. I think they weren't having a good time on the cruise and used us as an excuse." Alice sighed, reaching out to snatch a piece of cheese from a waiting platter.

"How can they not like a Mediterranean cruise?" CeCe asked. She was perched on the office chair, shaping a ball of dough with her swollen fingers. She'd long since given up attempts of wearing her wedding rings and was donned in the biggest tunic the restaurant supply store had. In an attempt to look festive, she tucked a spring of holly behind her ear.

Anthony and Alice shared matching expressions of *Have you met our parents*, when Natalie laughed. "I think they described it as a germ factory that floats. I have a feeling their cruising days are over."

Evan looked down at the ham he was glazing and shrugged. "We totally have enough food for four more. I mean, how much do four senior citizens eat anyway?"

"We're fine," CeCe said from her spot. "Although I would love another lower back rub and that canister of flour over there."

Evan held up honey-covered hands and grimaced. "Give me a minute, babe."

Alice went into action, wiggling her fingers. "I can handle the back rubs. I think we can all agree my culinary prowess isn't needed in this kitchen."

James rubbed his hands together, looking around the crowded space. "What can I do?"

Max hefted a turkey from the chiller and dropped it on the counter, the reverberating thud echoed around the crowded kitchen. "I'm about to get intimate with this bird. Do you mind going around and setting the tables? The kids can help if they're getting restless."

"I'll create a masterpiece." James spread his arms and beamed. He'd chosen a festive navy blue sweater dotted with miniature snowflakes that Alice had picked up as a present from Frick and Frack. There was also a red lipstick smear from his wife on his cheek, but no one was mentioning that. "Leave the tables to me," he said with a wink as he backed into the dining room.

Alice dug her heel into the small of CeCe's back, earning sounds that were certainly not appropriate for the kitchen. "Good Lord, woman. I can't tell if I'm hurting you or helping you."

Evan snorted, wiping his hands off before sprinkling the hams with brown sugar and mustard powder. "I've heard those sounds, and I assure you she was having a good time."

"Eww, gross, Ev." Mallory spluttered from the back door. Mallory and Maybelle had matching braids, their cheeks rosy from the cold.

Beckett followed her in, Maybelle's carrier hanging from his free arm. The other held several bags, which he hastily dropped by the counter. "Merry Christmas, everyone."

Natalie clapped, pushing him out of the way to get to Maybelle. "There's that little red-headed wonder. Come to Auntie Natalie."

Before anyone could blink, she had the baby in her arms and was covering her in kisses. "Please don't get any ideas, Nat," Anthony teased, but his eyes were filled with hearts as he gently tugged on the baby's braid.

Natalie tossed her head back and laughed, startling little Maybelle. "Oh, honey, don't you worry. I'm pretty sure at this point, my ovaries are dust."

CeCe balled up a piece of dough and threw it at Natalie, where it landed on her forehead before falling on the floor. "You could have a dozen more babies if you wanted, young lady."

Anthony looked torn between agreeing with CeCe and saving himself from a growing brood. "Technically, yes," he said, ever the politician.

Natalie cradled Maybelle and cooed to her before responding. "Everyone can relax. I just want a little Maybelle time."

Mallory sighed. "You're on baby duty all day as far as I'm concerned. Our little elf didn't realize that sleep is important, even on Christmas day."

Beckett groaned. "She had us up three times before dawn, so we gave up and did presents at five o'clock."

Max chuckled, his arm shoved up the turkey to his elbow. "Welcome to fatherhood, Beckett. It's fabulous, even when it's not."

The group went back to their varied tasks, with Alice and Mallory taking turns rubbing CeCe's back as she rolled out bread dough and the beginnings of a pie crust. "Are you sure you can handle all this?" Mallory whispered, concerned her sister-in-law was overdoing it.

CeCe's pinched expression didn't prove much either way, but she kept her head down and focused on her dough balls. "As I told my loving husband"—she paused to look over at Evan, who was currently browning mushrooms—"I feel great and want to bake. The babies are fine. I am fine." She raised a hand to pat her lower back. "Well, one of you needs to get to rubbing, then I'll be fine."

Mallory snorted. "I'm on it."

A few minutes later, James stuck his head through the kitchen door, a worried expression on his face. "Heya," he said to no one in particular.

Max was the first to look up. "What's up, man?"

James stepped inside, allowing the door to swing shut behind him. He rubbed the back of his neck and took a deep breath. "Remember how you were saying the more the merrier?"

Alice heard him, stopping her turn on operation save CeCe's back. "What's up, babe?"

James forced a grin and stepped back, opening the door to reveal not one but two unexpected guests. "Merry freaking Christmas!" Addison exclaimed as she bounded into the kitchen, a very embarrassed-looking Chloe bringing up the rear. "Got room for two more?"

CHAPTER 10
Turkeys and hams a plenty ...

Alice screamed, closing the distance and wrapping Addison in a firm embrace. "Oh my God, Addy." Behind them, Chloe shuffled her feet, clearly concerned they were interrupting a private party.

James draped his arm over her shoulder and pulled her into the fray. "Everyone, you all remember Addison's partner, Chloe." He waved his free hand around the kitchen, and added, "You remember everyone."

Chloe raised her hand to the group and, in a quiet voice, said, "Merry Christmas." Through her honey-colored skin, a blush crept up her neck. She hated being the center of attention on a good day, unlike her very boisterous girlfriend.

Max quickly washed his hands and extended one to Chloe. "It's great to see you again, Chloe. You and Addison are more than welcome. Pull up a seat and make yourself comfortable."

"Are you sure you have enough food?" Chloe asked, her expression pinched.

Addison joined Chloe, entwining their hands. "If Max says we're fine, we're fine."

James nodded, looking more relaxed. "He's an honest man. He wouldn't say it if he didn't mean it."

"James is right," Ginny perked up from her side of the kitchen. She'd washed a half dozen heads of lettuce for salads and was ready for a break. "How about I take you ladies out to the dining room? I was just about to start playing bartender."

"Then you are the woman to follow," Addison teased. Chloe trailed her girlfriend into the dining room as closely as a shadow.

Alice pulled James to the side of the kitchen and hissed. "Did you know they were coming? I feel terrible I didn't get them any gifts."

James held up his hands in surrender. "I'm as surprised as you are, seriously. When I was setting the table, I heard a knock on the window and saw them standing there. Chloe looked like she wanted to have the earth swallow her whole, but you know Addy. She was practically knocking the door down for some small-town cheer."

"Then that's what we'll give them," Max said from the stove. He'd moved into stuffing mode, toasting pieces of bread that CeCe had baked the day before.

"Plus, they're teeny tiny. I can't imagine those two eating that much," CeCe suggested, struggling to roll out her pie dough. "Damn this belly," she griped, twisting and turning in an effort to reach across the counter. The odd motions caused the holly behind her ear to fall to the floor, another casualty of her growing belly.

Evan lowered the heat on his burner and walked over to CeCe. "All right, champ, take a real seat." He put his hands on her shoulders and hustled her out into the dining room. Before everyone arrived, Evan set up a booth just for CeCe. There was her favorite back pillow, a stack of her favorite snacks at the ready, and her oversized water bottle.

"But I need to get those crusts in the oven by one o'clock, or we're not eating dessert."

Evan cupped CeCe's cheeks in his hands, staring into

her eyes for longer than was polite in mixed company. "Babe," he said, low so only CeCe could hear, "I love you." He leaned in and kissed her chastely on the lips. "I also love our babies." He placed his hands protectively over her swollen belly. "It's also Christmas, so that's even more reason to enjoy the moment. Sit, chat with your friends, and relax. Today, we actually have enough cooks in the kitchen."

Natalie joined them at the booth, sliding opposite CeCe and sipping from a glass of wine. "What happened to Maybelle?" CeCe asked, temporarily distracted. Evan took his chance and darted back to the kitchen.

Swirling her merlot, Natalie shrugged. "Maddie and Josie were dying for a chance to play with her, and Ginny got the bar set up so I got distracted."

CeCe snorted. "I'm guessing this means baby fever is over."

Natalie sipped from her glass and winked. "I think it wasn't really baby fever. Maybe a baby fever dream?" She placed her glass on the table and sighed contently. "Besides, I'm enjoying my forties and this bottle of vino too much to get knocked up again."

From across the aisle, Anthony cupped his hands in front of his mouth and shouted, "Thank the good Lord for that Christmas miracle."

Natalie flashed him a cheeky grin before turning back to her friend. "Speaking of baby fever, how are you holding up?"

CeCe pulled her water bottle closer and took a long swig. "I'm being held hostage by my own body." She patted her belly for full effect. "My husband is following me around like I'm a ticking time bomb."

Natalie grimaced. "You kind of are."

"I'm not due for another month, so simmer down, ma'am."

Natalie drained her glass and stood. "I'm getting a refill. You look like you need something. How about a little mocktail? Chloe is a miracle worker with the bar."

CeCe rearranged herself with her pillow and groaned. "Could you see if she has anything to put me into early labor? Like an old fashion or something?"

Natalie's smile slid away as she crouched in front of her friend. "What's going on there?" She reached out and covered one of CeCe's hands with her own. "That doesn't look like normal discomfort."

CeCe's eyes flashed with pain, but she didn't make a sound. "I've been having these little pains off and on all week. I'm sure it's holiday stress and my general hatred of being told what to do." She stuck her tongue out at Natalie, but she didn't get the response she wanted.

The flushed cheeks from her glass of wine melted into a worrisome shade of white. "I'm going to grab Mallory. She can give us her professional opinion."

"No!" CeCe shouted, snatching Natalie's hand and holding her in place. "Please, let's just leave this alone. I'm sure it's nothing, and I don't want to stress Evan out. It's Christmas."

"And I'm sure watching his wife grimace through her turkey dinner will make him the happiest elf in the land." Natalie pulled free and lowered her voice. "I'll tell Mallory to be discrete, but I'm getting her."

Natalie strode over the counter, her voice low in Mallory's ear. A moment later, the duo returned to the booth. Ever the professional, Mallory gave nothing away, save for a small frown. Her voice low, she asked, "Describe the pain to me. Is it constant or coming in waves?"

Natalie hovered in front of them, shielding them from the room. Raising her voice, she shouted toward the bar, "Can we get Momma CeCe a little something festive?" Her smile was tight, but she got a thumbs-up from Chloe.

"Still want that old fashion," CeCe chirped, earning a pinch from Mallory.

"Yeah, I don't think so. It's Christmas, not an alternate universe."

Chloe arrived, handing CeCe a mocktail the color of

sunshine. "I hope you like it," she said, chin dipped low. "It's mostly orange juice, but I wanted you to feel included. I used to make these to help out the DDs when I worked as a bartender."

CeCe took a break from her impromptu medical visit to thank the other woman and take a sip. "This is really good. Thanks, Chloe. I'm so glad you guys could join us."

Addison joined them, throwing her arm around Chloe's waist. "My girl is amazing when it comes to cocktails. Just give her one idea and she's off to the races." Chloe relaxed into Addison's hold, her pensive expression melting away.

Alice joined them, frowning when she saw Mallory on her knees in front of CeCe. "What's all this?" she asked loudly.

Natalie took her arm and tugged her back. "Shh, it's nothing."

Addison raised an eyebrow. "Alice. Why don't you tell Chloe about your book signing in Toronto?"

Alice's eyes darted back and forth until she agreed. "Sure, but only if you tell me about that kid you helped get into Harvard. James was telling me about it, but he's no storyteller. I need all the details." Their trio stalked off to another booth, leaving Natalie and Mallory to continue their baby talk.

Mallory placed her fingers on CeCe's wrist, checking her pulse before lowering her voice. "I always keep a portable blood pressure cuff in my car. I'm going to dip out the back and grab it, you stay here."

CeCe made to get up, but Natalie placed her hand on her shoulder. "Sit still. The more you move around, the more obvious it is that something is going on."

CeCe deflated back into her seat and scowled. "I'm never getting pregnant again," she muttered.

Mallory strode into the kitchen, being careful to keep her gaze off her brother. If Evan suspected anything was up, he'd turn into a tornado of anxiety. She spotted Beckett helping James fold cloth napkins in the far counter, and she snagged his eye.

"You mind if I take a quick break?" Beckett asked, holding up a sad excuse for a flower. The fabric wilted in his grasp, a limp ball of linen.

James blinked at the bundled fabric and winced. "Yeah, man. No problem. I've got it." Casting a look over his shoulder at Mallory, he added, "Take your time."

Beckett hesitated a moment before comparing his monstrosity with James's artfully folded lotus flowers. James may work primarily in paints, but he could certainly give napkin artists a run for their money—if that profession even exists. "Thanks," he mumbled before following his wife outside.

As soon as she stepped into the cold air, Mallory exhaled. Beckett closed the door behind them and caught up to his wife in two strides. "What's going on?" he asked, taking her hand and squeezing, snowflakes already coating his red hair.

"Hopefully nothing," she whispered, opening the trunk and pulling out a tote bag.

Beckett blanched at the sight of her medical kit. "Oh boy, what's going on?" His eyes grazed over his wife from head to toe. "I'm guessing this isn't for you."

Mallory looked over her shoulder again to ensure they were alone. "It's CeCe. I think she might be in labor."

"Holy crap." Beckett gasped, rocking back on his heels. "Should we call an ambulance?"

Shaking her head, Mallory hoisted the bag up her shoulder. "I don't think we're there yet. I want to check her blood pressure and a few other things." Lowering her voice further, she added, "And needless to say, don't say a freaking word to Ev. He'll lose his mind."

Beckett mimicked zipping his mouth shut and nodded. "Let me go in first, just in case he sees you with your bag. Ev's distracted, but he's not an idiot."

Mallory huffed out a laugh. "Great idea."

But a distraction wasn't needed, as a parade of Buckeyes

marched up the parking lot. "Hold the door," Helen shouted, waving her hands over her head. Mallory hardly recognized the older woman outside her diner uniform. She looked smart in a red pantsuit, her gray hair swept back in a bun.

"Helen? Trudy?" Mallory's head whipped toward their new mayor. "Mayor Josh?"

The group surrounded Beckett and Mallory, each wearing different expressions. "Hey," Josh said, awkwardly waving. "We uh, had a change in plans with Christmas." He was clad in a suit that seemed two sizes too big, the fabric hanging off his young frame. Trudy was dressed for a day at the office in a charcoal dress and a green cardigan.

Trudy huffed, reaching out to pinch his earlobe. "What my grandson is saying"—she sighed with the annoyance only a loving grandmother could provide—"is he made reservations for a hoity-toity Christmas dinner in Columbus, which is an hour away."

Helen helped her friend, nodding with each word. "And neither one of us wants to die on Route 70 because he's craving a steak."

The younger man flushed but soldiered on. "I know the diner isn't *technically* open," he hedged, his tone slipping into politics, "but Helen mentioned Max was hosting his friends and family, and aren't we really all like family?"

Mallory opened her mouth to respond when Anthony opened the back door. "Everything okay out here?" His question faltered when he caught sight of the new arrivals. "Trudy?" He stomped down the steps and welcomed his former assistant with a warm hug. "What are you doing here?" He looked quickly to Josh before lowering his voice. "I thought you were going to Columbus tonight?"

Trudy rolled her eyes. "I'm not dying today, Anthony."

Anthony shook his head, stifling a laugh. "I'm not sure I follow."

Josh stepped closer, pulling his shoulders back, trying to look like an authority figure in the presence of his predecessor. "I'm willing to drive, but Grandma and Helen are convinced the roads are too bad."

"Hello?" Helen asked, flapping her arms around at the still falling snow. "It's a blizzard, Joshy."

Josh's ears burned crimson, and he hissed. "Aunt Helen, can you please stop calling me Joshy? I'm the mayor."

"Mayor-Elect," Trudy corrected, offering her grandson another eye roll. Turning back to her former boss, she added, "Do you think you guys have room for three more?"

Anthony didn't hesitate, nodding and holding his arm out for them to follow him inside. "Absolutely, c'mon in. The more the merrier."

"That is how you handle a problem, Joshy," Trudy said, linking her arm through his and following Anthony.

As soon as they stepped inside, Max greeted everyone and ushered them out to a table. "I'm tempted to flip the sign to *Open* at this rate," he teased, sliding a casserole into the oven.

Anthony raked his hands through his hair, grimacing. "I'm sorry, man. I panicked when I saw them."

Max shook his head. "It's fine, really."

Evan agreed, squeezing a lemon over a tray of brussels sprouts. "We have more than enough."

Anthony deflated. "Thanks. I just didn't want to look weak in front of"—he did air quotes—"Mayor Josh."

Max snorted. "You realize he was only elected because you're leaving, right? If you wanted to stay a lowly local mayor, it would have been no contest, Representative Snyder."

Anthony nodded. "I know that, but it doesn't mean I like that Joshy is going to be sitting in my seat. I used to chase him out of the breakroom for stealing Snickers from the vending machine."

"You should have mentioned that during his campaign." Evan laughed at his own joke while he washed his hands. "No one wants a thief running city hall."

Mallory and Beckett managed to squeak past Evan and

make it to CeCe without anyone noticing. The new trio of diners was the perfect distraction as they settled into their own booth.

"Would you please stop fussing, grandma?" Josh asked as Trudy attempted to smooth back his collar. Her gnarled fingers dug into his skin as she righted his wrinkled shirt.

"We don't want you looking this sloppy with voters present," Trudy assured him, licking her thumb to swipe off a perceived smudge from his cheek.

Helen snorted. "He's already won the election, Trudy. Let the boy keep what's left of his dignity."

"Thank you?" Josh said, balling up his coat and using it as a buffer to his well-meaning grandmother.

"This is already more fun than a snooty steakhouse in Columbus," Helen quipped, taking a cocktail from Chloe.

Two booths away, Beckett ushered Mallory into place with CeCe. Once his wife was covered, his gaze swept the dining room for their daughter. "Should I go get Maybelle?"

Mallory shook her head, gesturing toward the far side of the room. Their baby was giggling while Maddie and Josie made silly faces, completely uninterested in her parents or the prospect of her next meal. "Let's leave her be for now. She'll get hungry or need a diaper change soon enough." She hooked her hand around Beckett's elbow, pulling him close for a peck on the cheek. "Thanks for your help."

"You don't need to thank me, but you're welcome. Now, let's figure out what's going on with CeCe." He pressed his lips to the shell of her ear, whispering words of admiration that only she could hear.

Natalie rose as Mallory opened her bag, moving over a pillow so she could sit next to CeCe. "Was that Trudy and our new mayor I just saw?"

"Yup," Mallory agreed, pulling out the blood pressure cuff and looping it through CeCe's arm. To hide what she was doing, she tossed the pillow in front of the mother-to-be. "If you want to go over there and distract them for a moment, I wouldn't say no."

Natalie took CeCe's empty juice glass. "I'm on it. Anyone need a drink on my way back?"

"Bourbon on the rocks would be great." CeCe beamed from her perch on pillow island. Her hands rested on her belly, the picture of serenity. The only crack in her restful image was her pinched expression.

Mallory checked the readings. "Don't talk, and try a few deep breaths for me. Beckett can go get you some juice if you'd like."

Before Natalie disappeared, she leaned in, and offered, "You need a ride out of here, our SUV has 4-wheel drive and my husband is still technically in charge." She winked, patting CeCe's knee in support.

"Thanks," CeCe said through clenched teeth.

Mallory pursed her lips at the reading and made a few notes on her phone. "When did the pain start?"

CeCe's eyes flicked around a moment in thought. "Technically, last night?"

Her response came out in a question, causing Mallory to scowl. "All right, Mr. Trebek. I don't need my answers in the form of questions. When did you start having discomfort? And be honest, or I'm getting my brother."

CeCe's eyes grew wide, and she shook her head. "Okay, I'll cooperate. Don't get Evan." She rested her hands on her belly and frowned. "I've noticed some *minor*"—she stressed the word—"contractions starting two days ago."

Mallory was incredulous. "Two days ago? That's when you stopped by the farm to see us. You were in pain then?"

"I've been in some form of pain since your brother knocked me up," CeCe said, wincing as a fresh round of contractions hit.

Mallory pulled herself up to standing, dusting off her knees. "Yeah, I'm getting the car. We're on our way to the hospital."

With a lightning-fast reaction neither woman expected, CeCe latched onto Mallory's wrist. "Sit down. I'm not going to be the reason Christmas is ruined."

Mallory tried to yank herself free, but CeCe's fingers dug into her skin. "Not to state the obvious, dear sister-in-law, but you'll ruin Christmas if you have a medical emergency during the turkey carving."

"Not. Going. To. Happen," CeCe clipped, a bead of sweat sliding down her temple. She looked at the clock over the door to the kitchen. "We have an hour until dinner will be ready. I'm going to sit here in my pillow fort and sip water. I will be fine. As soon as the pie is served, I'll ask Ev to take me."

Mallory's head fell back in exasperation. "You know this is a horrible idea, right?"

"Never said it was a good idea, just the right one for the moment."

Pinching the bridge of her nose, Mallory collected her thoughts. She looked down at her phone where CeCe's blood pressure and heart rates were documented. "Your water hasn't broken yet?"

CeCe quickly shook her head. "See? I'm going to be okay." She protectively covered her belly with her hands. "These babies are fine. Just a little restless."

"I'm going to regret this," Mallory said, stepping back. "I'll give you turkey, but you're not sitting here through dessert."

CeCe's head bobbed in agreement. "Fair compromise."

Beckett appeared with Maybelle on his hip. In a hushed tone, he said, "I can have the car up at the door in sixty seconds. What's the plan?"

Mallory leaned in and reiterated what CeCe and she decided.

"Lawless will hate that plan."

"Which is why you're not going to say a word, Foxy." CeCe glared, causing the redhead to squirm.

"Please don't scare my husband," Mallory warned. "You're trying to stay on my good side, remember?"

CeCe blew raspberries, causing Maybelle to giggle. "Fine, but only because you have me by the balls."

"Merry Christmas to us all," Mallory droned, pinching Maybelle's cheeks and earning a giggle of her own. "Operation hide CeCe will commence, but I'm the general of this operation. If I think you need to go, you listen to me. Okay?"

CeCe saluted. "Aye-aye, Captain."

"You're messing with my analogies, but thank you." She pointed to CeCe, and added, "Don't make me regret it."

CHAPTER 11
Merry Christmas, from two of Santa's elves

One hour, several gallons of cocktails (and mocktails), and a cheese board later, Max paraded out of the kitchen with the biggest turkey anyone had ever seen. The bird weighed approximately three tons and was the perfect golden hue. He placed it at the edge of the counter where he artfully carved it, lining up the slices on a platter better than Martha Stewart. Evan came out a moment later with the ham, studded with cloves and smelling like a sweet and savory dream.

Ginny carried out several bowls of potatoes and vegetables, with Helen helping with the various cranberry sauces. Ginny tried to swat the older woman away. "Would you stop, Helen? You're not on the clock."

"Pfft, but I'm a party crasher. It's the least I can do."

Alice popped up and smacked a kiss on Helen's cheek. "You're not crashing, and Ginny's right, you're not on the clock. Unless you want to get me a ginger ale." She winked and Helen sighed.

"I can't wait to retire."

Mona walked out of the kitchen with several baskets of CeCe's freshly baked rolls. They were the size of softballs and glistened with their buttery glaze. "I'm sorry to hear you're retiring, Helen. Hopefully you'll have some time to join us at the community center for Pickleball. Harold and I are getting pretty good."

Alice took the baskets from Mona and placed them at the end of the buffet. "Hush, Mona. I'm trying to talk Helen into delaying retirement."

Helen grunted. "You need to let this go, kid." Alice opened her mouth to argue, but Helen placed a finger over her lips. "Ho, ho, ho." She winked and stomped off toward Trudy, who was gesturing her over with a bottle of wine she'd stolen from the bar.

The kids all lined up first, greedy expressions on their faces. "Can I have the wishbone?" Henry asked, leaning into Mona's side. He knew where to get what he wanted; his grandmother was helpless to stop him.

"Hen, let's get everyone served first." Max was all business, ensuring everyone had plates. Evan assisted until Max shooed him away. "Go check on your wife, we've got this."

Evan didn't need to be told twice, side-stepping the line to get to CeCe's booth. As he strode to the table, he beamed. "Babe, I'm so proud of you. You stayed put all afternoon." He kissed her forehead and muttered some endearing words before catching her gaze.

"You know me," CeCe said through clenched teeth. She leaned into the contraction, struggling to keep her tone even.

Misunderstanding her pain for annoyance at being kicked out of her own kitchen, Evan offered, "Can I make you a plate? You seem so comfortable here, I'd hate to move you." He tucked a loose lock of hair behind her ear, the look in his eyes nothing short of besotted.

CeCe made to sit up, turning so her feet hit the floor. Mallory joined them before she could stand, holding her hand out. "I've got this. What do you want?"

At first, CeCe protested, but Mallory shot her a look that

stopped her objections. "Just a little of everything?"

Mallory nodded, but added, "Only the pregnancy-approved foods. Got it."

"You're the best, Mal." Evan sat with CeCe and leaned down to kiss her belly. "This might be my favorite Christmas yet. Everyone's all together, the diner is cozy, the snow is gorgeous, and the meal looks perfect."

"Watch it, mister," CeCe chided. "I only cooked a few things. It can't possibly be perfect." She frowned, and this time it was for more than unwanted contractions. CeCe reveled in any opportunity to be in the kitchen. Missing out on the final touches of this feast zapped what was left of her Christmas cheer.

The buffet line was under control, so Max grabbed a napkin and set of utensils for CeCe. Following Mallory, he handed it to his friend. "Easy, CeCe. I know you're pregnant, but now you're hurting my feelings."

She raised an eyebrow at her boss. "Did you remember to put the Dijon mustard in the gravy?"

Max covered his heart with his hand. "Wow, it's like you forgot I went to culinary school. Ouch."

Mallory slid the plate over to CeCe, who immediately tucked in. Apparently being in labor did nothing to squash her appetite. "Thank you," she said through a mouthful of roasted parsnips.

"Yeah, yeah," Mallory muttered, walking away to find Beckett and Maybelle. There were a few things the little carrot top could eat, and she was eager to have some quality time with her favorite duo. Plus, she needed a distraction from a potential medical emergency happening on her watch. Keeping CeCe here went against everything she learned in school, yet she felt stuck.

"You're sure she's all right?" Beckett asked, mashing up a square of sweet potato on his plate before handing it to Maybelle.

Mallory's heart clenched at the sight, how effortlessly her husband took the lead with Maybelle. She was one lucky lady, and she planned on showing Beckett how lucky when they managed a moment alone.

"She's going to be peachy. Let's eat." The lie slipped off her tongue so easily, Mallory could almost believe it.

At the table across from them, Alice, James, Addison, and Chloe animatedly discussed the happenings in New York.

James speared a carrot with his fork and asked, "So, Chloe, you're still enjoying the nonprofit?"

Chloe sipped from her wine and nodded, cheeks pink from the libations. "Yes, I really do. I won't lie, there's moments I wonder why I gave up serving and bartending." She chuckled at Addison's expression. "But I knew I needed something beyond waiting tables. It was a good gig, but I was never around for Addy's events, and the hours were killing me. Now I get to help people and have more time for this one here." She tipped her head toward Addison before sneaking a roasted potato from her plate.

Addison pretended to be outraged by the food theft, but that didn't last long. She reached out and smoothed back Chloe's collar, pulling her close for a chaste kiss. "I won't lie, I'm loving your new schedule. Although I do miss the hook-up for free dim sum."

"Did the restaurant close?" James asked, already frowning at the loss of his beloved dumpling spot in New York. It had been a favorite place of his and Addison's when they both lived in the city. He'd loved it for the food, and Addison had loved it for her favorite waitress. After one too many visits without making a move, Addison had left her phone number on a receipt, and the rest was history.

Chloe shook her head. "No. Believe it or not, restaurants can continue operating when one of the servers leaves."

Alice grimaced. "Let's hope, otherwise Helen retiring will end the diner as we know it."

"You need to let it go!" Helen barked from three tables away. She winked before turning back to a very fascinating story Mayor Josh was telling about a time in college when he sweet-talked his buddy out of a speeding ticket.

Meanwhile, the kids had taken over the corner booth. Otis and Henry were involved in a ham eating contest while Josie and Madeline made a Jenga set from a collection of sugar packets.

Mona and Harold shared a table with Trudy, Mayor Josh, Helen, Donna, and Steven. While none of them were where they expected to be this Christmas, they could not deny they were in a pretty good place. Plus, Mona was enraptured by Josh's storytelling abilities. Harold privately wondered if the kid was old enough to vote for himself, let alone run the town.

Max turned up the music, so Bing Crosby could serenade them over dinner. Ginny took his hand and ushered him back to his seat so he could enjoy the fruits of his labor. "This is all delicious. I think you and Evan outdid yourselves."

Anthony and Natalie slid across from them, their plates stacked embarrassingly high. "No arguments here. I only wish I would have worn my sweatpants so I could eat more." Natalie wore a red dress that fit her curves and flared out just below her knees. Despite the falling snow, she'd worn a favorite pair of kitten heels to finish off her festive ensemble.

"Yeah, right. I'm calling BS on that one, Nat. Your sweatpants haven't seen the light of day in eons."

Natalie pursed her lips a moment before agreeing. "Yeah, you're right. There's also no way I wouldn't take any excuse to show off my festive dress." She shimmied in her seat, earning a stolen kiss from Anthony.

"You're gorgeous," he assured her, reaching under the table to squeeze her knee.

"This is the perfect send-off to this place," Ginny said through a mouthful of ham. Max let out a shuddering breath but nodded. "I don't want to be a wet blanket," she assured the table, hoping her voice didn't waiver, "it's just that we've had some wonderful moments here. I know we'll reopen again, but it won't be exactly the same."

Max quipped, "Yeah, the booths won't be lumpy and the counters won't be cracked."

Anthony gestured with his fork. "I personally love the lumps."

"I'm with Ginny," Natalie said, nudging her husband aside so she could steal his dinner roll. "This is perfect."

"You're all right. It's a little bittersweet, but it's also time. Not everything can stay the same. Isn't that right, Representative Snyder?"

Everyone laughed and went back to discussing the food.

Natalie had managed to stay distracted for a few minutes, and Ginny, Max, and Anthony didn't notice how often her gaze kept sneaking off to CeCe's booth. She was nibbling on her dinner, and Evan didn't seem concerned. When her gaze reached Mallory, both women rolled their eyes. Apparently they were the only two worried about the mother-to-be.

By the time everyone cleaned their plates, it was time to bring out the desserts. Max joined Evan at their table, and asked, "Can I borrow you a minute to grab all the pies and cookies?"

CeCe held up a hand. "I want to help. I went to all that trouble and, frankly, my feet are asleep."

Evan took her hand as she slid free from the booth. "I'll help you up, but you're not stepping foot in that kitchen. Stretch your legs, but relax. We've got this."

CeCe whined, "But I hate being so helpless."

Max snorted. "CeCe, you baked two pie crusts and made cheesy bites. You've already done too much."

"Yeah, yeah." CeCe huffed as she shuffled toward the kitchen door. Just as she stepped behind the counter, she doubled over, clutching her belly and letting out a low moan.

Mallory was on her feet and by her side before Evan registered what was going on. "CeCe, talk to me," Mallory ordered.

Before CeCe could say a word, a splash of something wet hit the floor. Misunderstanding what had happened, Evan snatched a stack of paper towels. "Careful, babe. Looks like someone spilled something."

Mallory scoffed, still shocked at her brother's obliviousness after all these years. "Her water just broke, you idiot." Raising her voice, she shouted to Beckett, "Need that car now, honey!"

Beckett was on his feet, running toward the exit with Maybelle in his arms, a trail of sweet potatoes sliding down her little chin. "It's baby time!" he said to a very confused Maybelle.

"Did you say baby time? Is CeCe okay?" Helen was on her feet, keeping pace as Beckett weaved around the other guests.

"Yes, erm, I think? I don't know, but I'm getting the car." He nearly toppled over his own shoes as Maybelle reached out and snatched his glasses with her chubby hand. While ordinarily the cutest thing, he didn't have the mental bandwidth to enjoy the interaction.

"Woah there," Harold said, holding up a hand and stopping Beckett in his tracks. "What do you need, son?"

Beckett blinked, suddenly unsure what the hell was going on. "Uh, I need to uh …"

Mona, ever a champ in a crisis, held out her arms for the baby. "We've got this, Uncle Beckett."

Harold patted his shoulder and smiled. "Between the two of us, we've raised three kids. Go get the car."

Helen nodded, pushing Beckett's other shoulder until he started to walk.

Still speechless, Beckett handed Maybelle off to Mona. He quickly kissed the baby's cheek before placing another kiss on Mona's cheek. "Thank you."

Evan's blue eyes grew wild as reality dawned. "Holy crap," he mumbled. "Is this? Are you? Are they coming, now?" With each question, his voice rose an octave. "Now? We're having babies, *now*?"

"Wow, I really thought he'd be better prepared for this," Mallory deadpanned, bumping her brother out of the way. "Yes, Ev. Your wife is in labor."

The ham eating contest and Jenga battles paused as the kids heard the commotion. "What's going on?" Otis shouted to no one in particular.

Henry was more concerned with the fact that the desserts were on the buffet line, and he shrugged as he sauntered over for his fifth helping of food. Josie and Madeline's level of concern was slightly higher, but it didn't stop them from snatching a few cookies on their way toward the chaos.

"C'mon, buddy," Natalie said as she took Henry by the elbow. "You guys sit tight while we get CeCe sorted out." Natalie ushered the kids back to their booth before shouting, "I need a mayor!"

Both Anthony and Josh perked up at her request, nearly knocking each other over as they ran to the back booth.

"What's up?" Josh asked, his eyes wide with excitement. "Do mayors deliver babies?" He rubbed his hands together, a blob of cranberry sauce falling from the cuff of his shirt.

Anthony didn't bother hiding his responding shudder. "No, Josh. That's not on the job description." Turning to Natalie, he asked, "What do you need?"

"Call the highway patrol and tell them we're speeding towards Buckeye Falls General in Beckett's car. I don't want anyone getting pulled over while CeCe's in labor."

Anthony pulled out his phone and nodded. "I'm on it." Turning to Josh, he said, "Watch and learn, Joshy."

Too stunned to reply, the younger man only followed Anthony as he strode away to make the calls.

Evan ran his hands through his blond hair again. His lips kept moving, but he wasn't making a sound. "So this is really happening? I thought we had another few weeks before it was … real?"

Mallory held CeCe steady while she found her footing. "Ev, I'd love to waste time going over the birds and the bees, but didn't Dad cover that twenty years ago? Once your birds populate CeCe's bees, you get a baby." Ginny snorted beside them, but rallied quickly.

CeCe wheezed as another round of contractions hit. She bared down, gripped Evan's arm with all her strength. "What your sister is trying to say"—she gasped for a fresh breath—"is that we're about to have two more uninvited guests at this celebration," CeCe said through clenched teeth.

Evan blanched, dragging his free hand down his face. "But it's too soon." Turning to Mallory, he asked, "It's too soon, right?" He looked around at the other stunned faces, hoping someone would have something helpful to add to the chaos unfolding around him. "They're going to be okay, right?" His voice finally broke, a single tear sliding down his cheek.

"Ev," CeCe said, her tone sharp but concerned. Evan snagged her gaze and blinked, willing his heart rate to slow so he could hear through the pounding in his ears. "I need you now, okay?"

Evan nodded dumbly, his Christmas feast doing somersaults through his belly. He was about to become a dad, and he was simultaneously thrilled and petrified. *Like any father ...*

Mallory slid from nurse mode to sister mode, snaking her hand around Evan's bicep and squeezing. "These babies are the bosses, little brother, and right now they're making the rules. You need to help your wife and kids."

That was all it took to snap Evan out of his panic-induced haze. "Holy crap," he repeated. "We're going to have some babies!" Turning to CeCe, he kissed her nose and grinned. "I love you."

CeCe cracked a smile in between contractions, her own eyes brimming with tears. "I love you, too. Can we go now?"

Evan nodded, a loose curl falling on his face. "Yeah, babe. We can go."

Outside they heard Beckett honk the horn. "That's our

ride," Mallory announced, taking CeCe's other arm and ushering the expectant parents toward the exit. Anthony held the door open, and said, "I just got off the phone with Jerry at the highway patrol. They have Beckett's license plate and won't pull you guys over. Congratulations."

"Thanks, man." Evan clapped his shoulder as they pushed through.

Behind them everyone cheered and offered their well wishes. Evan opened the backseat for CeCe, but was stopped from joining her by Mallory. "Hop up front with Beckett. I want to be here in case there's any funny business."

"Like what?"

"In case one of them tries to pop out, I'll push them back in." Mallory scoffed, her voice dripping with sarcasm. "Just get in the front seat, Ev."

Beckett tapped the horn again, startling Evan into the moment. "Take shotgun, Lawless. I need you to navigate."

Evan bent down to cup CeCe's cheek, running his thumb over the soft skin. "Are you okay?" he whispered, his voice brimming with emotions.

"I'm fine. Just do as Mal and Beckett say." She winked, and he finally got into his seat.

Mallory held CeCe's hand and coached her through the contractions.

Anthony was true to his word. As soon as Beckett merged onto the highway, a police cruiser turned on his lights and led the way toward the hospital. "It's good to know people," Beckett said as he followed the police car. "I've never been in a police escort," he marveled.

Mallory blinked. "Oh my God. Who has Maybelle?"

Evan snorted. "Real nice, Mal. You misplaced your baby and you're giving me guff."

Beckett punched Evan in the shoulder, still keeping the car steady in the snow. "She's with Harold and Mona. They offered, and I was too worked up to argue."

"Oh, phew," Mallory said with her hand on her heart.

"She couldn't be in better hands."

"Agreed, now hold on, because here comes our exit." Beckett eased the car off the highway and angled it toward the hospital, which was just ahead. "Hang in there, CeCe. You're killing it."

"I love you so much, babe," Evan said, tears falling down his cheeks.

"Love you"—CeCe let out a yelp of pain—"too."

"Do something, Mal!" Evan shouted, pointing at his wife with a look of terror in his eyes.

"I'm doing everything I can, and so is CeCe. Beckett, pull up to the ER entrance. They're expecting us."

Beckett pulled up just as Evan threw his door open and ran into the hospital. "We're having a baby!" he shouted, frantically looking around for help. The lobby was full of folks who had had their own versions of exciting Christmases. A young man held what looked like a broken arm to his chest, while an older woman coughed into a handkerchief. A tired-looking receptionist didn't look up from her workstation.

"Hello!? I said we're having a baby!" Evan linked his hands together and waved them side to side, as if rocking a baby to sleep. "My wife is having twins right now!"

Mallory ran in after him, fortunately able to be calm in high-stress situations. She strode up to the check-in desk and smiled politely at the receptionist. "Hi there, and Merry Christmas."

The other woman looked up and smiled. "Merry Christmas. What seems to be the problem?"

Evan slammed his hand down on the desk, but Mallory cut him off. "My sister-in-law is in labor, she's just outside. She's a month early, carrying twins, BP is slightly elevated, but there was no blood loss and her contractions are less than two minutes apart. Water broke about fifteen minutes ago."

Evan blinked beside her, shaking in his sneakers. "Thanks, Mal." He fell against her side, his knees wobbly.

Mallory wrapped an arm around his waist, keeping him from collapsing in a heap.

"Deep breaths, Ev. You're about to meet your children." She kissed his sweaty forehead and turned him in the direction of the car. "Let's roll."

A nurse joined them with a wheelchair and followed them out to the car. The police officer helped get CeCe settled before he went on his way. Beckett parked the car in the lot before running after the group, his shoes slipping on ice patches the entire way inside.

When he came back, Mallory was slumped on a chair by the elevators. Her braid was limp, whisps of hair flying out in all directions. "They won't let me go up until she's been given a room."

Beckett fell to his knees, taking Mallory's shaking hands in his. "She's going to be fine, and so are those babies." Kissing each of her knuckles, he added, "And you were spectacular with her. You continue to amaze me."

Mallory didn't respond, just took even breaths as she tried to slow her own racing heart. "I know, but I'm still terrified."

"She's a Lawson-in-law. You're a tough group." He adjusted his glasses, which were askew and smudged from the last half hour of excitement. Mallory detected small fingerprints courtesy of their daughter.

"Thanks for the ride, speed racer."

"Anything for Lawless and my future niece and nephew."

Mallory scrunched her nose. "How do you know it's one of each? Evan and CeCe aren't telling us a thing."

Beckett shrugged. "It's obvious, isn't it? They struggled for so long to get pregnant. I just feel like the universe should cooperate and give them one of each."

"I can't argue with that logic." Mallory pulled Beckett into her arms, burrowing her face in the crook of his neck. She took in a pull of his comforting cedar scent and promised herself that everyone would be all right. It was

Christmas, and their little family deserved a miracle.

Three hours later, Evan joined them in the waiting room. He simultaneously looked elated and exhausted; both Mallory and Beckett heaved a sigh of relief. "So? What's the verdict?" Mallory asked, leaping from her seat.

Evan's trademark grin lit up his face. "We've got a healthy son *and* daughter. Mommy's doing fine."

Beckett punched the air and whooped. "I knew it!"

Mallory pulled her brother into a firm hug, tears already cascading down her face. "Congratulations."

"What are their names?" Beckett asked, joining the group hug.

Evan pulled back and wiped his eyes with his sleeves. "Charlie and Eva." CeCe's father's name had been Charles, and Eva was a clear nod to her father.

"Perfect names," Beckett said.

"For perfect babies," Mallory added.

For a moment, the trio stood and sobbed in a mixture of joy and relief. "When can we see CeCe?" Mallory asked.

"You took the words right out of our mouths," Max said, striding in with Ginny, Natalie, and Anthony right behind him.

Evan's grin grew at the sight of his friends. "What are you doing here?" he asked as Max pulled him in for a hug. The two men had known each other for over a decade, yet Evan didn't think he'd ever been so happy to see his boss and mentor. He leaned into the embrace and felt the solid reassurance of another father. If Max could handle fatherhood, so could he.

Natalie huffed. "Like you could keep us away."

Ginny nodded, pulling Evan into a quick hug of her own. "As soon as we got everything cleaned up, we were too restless to wait." She turned to Beckett and Mallory. "Maybelle is at my dad's place with the rest of the kids. Mona still has her own car seat from her granddaughter, so everyone is safe and happy. Alice and James send their best. They took Chloe and Addison back to their place."

Max grimaced. "Although I'm already afraid Henry ate your folks out of house and home."

Anthony was incredulous. "I watched that kid eat half a ham just two hours ago."

"Forget Zippy, I think Henry can beat any eating contest."

Everyone laughed, falling into their usual rapport.

Suddenly Evan shook his head and laughed. "Holy crap, I'm a father. I gotta go." Turning to Mallory, he asked, "Can you call Sophie and Emily? I called Mom and Dad on the elevator ride."

Mallory shot a thumbs-up. "I'm on it. Will you text us when CeCe is ready for visitors?"

Evan grinned. "Absolutely."

"Congratulations, Lawless," Beckett said again, cuffing his friend on the shoulder.

The others shouted their congratulations and well wishes, causing a scene in a fairly quiet waiting room.

Evan blinked back a fresh round of tears. "I love you guys. I love everyone today! Merry Christmas, Buckeye Falls!"

And with that, Evan hopped in the elevator to rejoin his wife and babies. In his thirty-six years on this planet, his sister had never seen him so happy. And for the happiest guy in town, that was certainly saying something.

CHAPTER 12
What's one more announcement?

"And the babies are both fine?" Chloe asked, fidgeting with the bangles on her wrist.

James nodded as he turned his car onto Main Street, one hand holding Alice's as the other steered to avoid a pothole. He swiped his thumb over her knuckles as he smiled. Even with all the chaos of the babies' arrival, it had been one of his favorite Christmases to date. "Yep. Just got a text from Anthony. Mommy and babies are fine, but don't ask me their names."

Alice threw her head back and laughed. "Are you serious? We just read the text as we left the diner. It's Eva and Charlie, both perfect names." Chloe and Addison *ooed* and *ahhed* from their spots in the back of the car.

The snow had finally slowed to the big fat flakes that were perfect for snow globes, the air crisp and cool. The clouds had dispersed, allowing the stars to twinkle and add another layer of magic to their drive home. Frankly, if the scenery got any more serene, James would have to lock himself away in his studio to create another masterpiece. He squashed his creative mojo, too eager to spend time with three of his favorite people.

Oblivious to her husband's musings, Alice quickly fired off a series of texts to both her brother and friends sharing their congratulations. Talk about a Christmas miracle!

After the bedlam of CeCe's labor, the vibes at the diner varied between excitement and trepidation. As soon as Anthony got word that everyone was okay, the holiday celebration continued as everyone chipped in to tidy up the diner and make sure everyone's kids and belongings were taken care of.

Unfortunately, the birth of the twins did little to crush Chloe's concerns that they were third and fourth wheels to the festivities. "Are you sure we can crash at your place?" Chloe asked from the back seat, feet bobbing in time with her racing heart.

Addison leaned against her, her head resting on her shoulders. "No, Chloe, they're going to make us sleep in the car." She gestured with her free hand out the window and chuckled. "Or worse, left on the mean streets of Buckeye Falls. I don't know if we'll survive the night."

Alice swung around in her seat and frowned. "Chloe, we've known you for nearly a decade. Can you please remember that we love you?"

James snickered from the driver's seat. "Sometimes more than Addy."

"Hey," Addison admonished, causing Chloe to giggle.

"Thank you. We weren't sure what we wanted to do for the holidays, and I suddenly got homesick for cliched Christmas traditions and some snow that wasn't gray from cabs and loud New Yorkers." Chloe hefted out a sigh that deflated her, causing her to melt into Addison's hold. "But then when CeCe went into labor, I started doubting we were where we needed to be."

"You're always welcome," James and Alice said in unison.

James pulled into the garage and helped the ladies with their luggage. Alice strode ahead to plug in the Christmas tree and start a pot of tea. "Anyone in the mood for a

Christmas movie and some tea?"

"That sounds heavenly," Addison agreed, tossing her bags in the guest room before falling onto the couch, limbs splayed all over three cushions. She made enough room for Chloe to join her, causing James to laugh.

"Wow, Addy. You really are a couch hog."

"You should see how she hogs the covers," Chloe teased.

James clapped. "I knew it! There was no way you weren't a blanket hog."

Addison pulled herself upright and eased back into one cushion. "All right, you've all made your points." She took Chloe's hand and kissed her palm. She whispered something only Chloe could hear, causing her to turn a worrisome shade of violet.

Alice emerged with a plate of cookies. "I managed to hide these from Otis." Behind them, the kettle sang its tune.

"I'll grab the tea. Everyone drinking?"

Chloe beamed. "Yes, please!"

Addison huffed. "Do you have anything stronger? We just witnessed the miracle of life, and, frankly, I need something to take the edge off."

Alice popped a cookie in her mouth and headed back to the kitchen. "That's actually a good point, Addy. I'm still drinking tea, but I might start with a little of the good stuff." She retrieved a nice vintage malbec and sauntered up to Addison.

"You open, I'll pour," Addison promised, lining up their glasses.

Chloe ate a cookie in silence, tucking her legs under herself. "I'm impressed, by everyone here."

James joined them, sliding mugs across the coffee table. "How so?"

"I don't know. I guess it's the sense of community. A woman's water broke in the middle of Christmas dinner, and everyone jumped to attention." She snapped her fingers. "Just like that. No hesitating, no pausing for selfies, you all just sprang into action."

Alice cocked her head. "In fairness, these were her friends and family."

"I think Chloe's right." Addison nodded, sipping from her glass. "This was more than friends helping friends. I felt like everyone stepped up without thinking."

"If that happened in New York, there'd be some asshole with their phone trying to go viral," Chloe said, with more venom than anyone expected.

"Wow, babes. I didn't know you were so against New Yorkers all of a sudden." Addison blinked in surprise.

Chloe shrugged, her attention back on the plate of cookies. "I don't hate New York, but sometimes I miss the quiet times." She gestured around her. "Like this, don't you just want to have a quiet life with your wife?"

At the mention of wives, both James and Alice stilled. Alice's eyes darted to her husband in a silent question of *Do you know something I don't?!*

James shook his head, nearly choking on a cookie. "You ladies want to tell us anything?"

Addison slowly sat up, knocking her cushion to the floor. "Chloe?"

Chloe looked at their friends before snagging Addison's gaze. "I, uh, wasn't going to say anything until we were alone."

"Oh my God!" Addison exclaimed, jumping to her feet and sprinting to the guestroom before anyone could breathe. Her footfalls disappeared down the hallway until they heard the door slam shut.

Alice, James, and Chloe all sat in stunned silence, their jaws on the floor. "I didn't think she'd literally run from the idea of marrying me," Chloe muttered, dropping her head to her chest. She took a few long breaths before reaching out for Addison's wine glass, downing it in two long gulps. With trembling fingers, she slid the glass back onto the coffee table and groaned. "I've been planning on proposing for years, and when I finally get the courage, I muck it up."

Alice wordlessly refilled the glass, pressing it into Chloe's hand. Turning to James, she mouthed, "What the hell do we do now?" James merely blinked in response, as if he'd swallowed his tongue.

Finally, the sound of a door opening echoed down the hall. Addison rejoined them in the living room. Her hands were balled into fists at her sides, her gaze anywhere but on Chloe.

For her part, Chloe looked mortified and took another pull from the wine glass. "Look, Addy, I shouldn't have ..." But her words were cut off as Addison strode forward, slowly dropping down to one knee.

"I will admit," Addison said, licking her lips and catching her breath, "I had a better plan than this." She brought her balled hand up and opened it, revealing a white gold band studded with emeralds, Chloe's birthstone.

Chloe gasped, covering her mouth with her hands. Her dark eyes shone with unshed tears. James and Alice mirrored her reaction. "Addy?"

"Chloe, I've been in love with you since the first time I ordered the tofu eggrolls. Since I left you my number you've calmed me, motivated me, and cherished me. I can only hope I've done the same for you." Lost for words, Chloe merely nodded. "So, the point of this is to say, would you do me the honor of being my wife? Let's find that cabin in the woods and live a beautiful life together?"

Chloe slid off the couch and got to her knees, now eye-level with Addison. "Absolutely, I'd be honored to be your wife." She held up a finger and fumbled in her cardigan pocket. "There's just one thing," she said as she pulled out a tiny velvet bag. Overturning the bag in her hand, a gold band with a solitaire diamond landed with a small thud. "I was going to ask you the same thing."

Before anyone could react, Alice screamed and jumped to her feet, sending her empty wine glass clattering to the floor. James hurriedly picked it up before tugging Alice onto his lap and shushing her. "Let them finish," he urged.

"Of course, sorry." Alice pursed her lips shut, her eyes darting back and forth between Addison and Chloe like she was watching a tennis match. She bounced like a child on Santa's knee until James pinched her elbow and stopped her fidgeting.

"Of my God." Addison panted, reaching out and sliding the ring on her fourth finger. "Yes, of course I'll marry you."

Both women giggled, staring at their rings in wonder. Chloe pulled Addison in for a kiss, while James and Alice tiptoed into the kitchen.

"Did you have any idea?" Alice stage-whispered to James.

"If I did, don't you think I would have said something?" He was incredulous. "I'm a terrible secret keeper, almost as bad as you."

Alice scoffed. "I'm not a bad secret keeper." She nibbled her lip a moment before bursting out into a fit of laughter. "Yeah, okay. We're both pretty bad at keeping secrets."

From the living room, Addison shouted, "You're both the worst!"

"Love you, too, Addy," James replied, tugging his wife closer.

"This is the best Christmas, ever." Alice melted against him, chasing his lips for a kiss.

"I have to agree. How about we give these two a little privacy? I have an idea."

Alice took his hand and followed her husband into the studio. The space was equipped with bright overhead lights, but for the holidays James had hung twinkle lights around the space. He turned them on now, ushering Alice to the far corner where a small loveseat waited for them.

While Alice got settled into her seat, James pulled a bottle of wine from one of their many travels. It was a special bottle they were saving for a special occasion. "We'll share with the girls in a minute, but first," he said, popping the cork and pouring two portions into old paint glasses, "a Christmas toast."

"I love you, you know that, right?" Alice teased, clinking glasses and opening her arms for James. He gracelessly fell onto the couch beside her, pulling her close until they were flush against each other. His heart rate slowed as they clicked into place. No matter where they were in the world, James never felt more at home than in Alice's arms.

"I love you more, Alice."

And there they sat, surrounded by twinkle lights in their creative space. To their left sat a bunch of James's completed canvases ready for their next showing. To their right was Alice's writing nook, her typewriter ribbon replaced, and a stack of paper at the ready. Despite all their journeys and adventures, Alice couldn't think of a better place to be for Christmas than right here, in Buckeye Falls with her husband, friends, and family.

CHAPTER 13
And babies make four …

"I don't want to point out the obvious," CeCe said from her perch in the hospital bed. The nurse had just taken the twins from the room for naptime, leaving Mommy and Daddy alone with only their thoughts and the reassuring beeps of the heart rate monitor.

"And what's that?" Evan asked, swiping her blonde hair back from her face. His fingers trailed down until he reached her shoulders. Giving a gentle squeeze, Evan leveled his blue gaze on his wife. Scratch that, on his amazing, life-giving wife. Evan was in pure awe of CeCe. *Not that that was out of the norm …*

CeCe took the plastic cup of ice chips off the side table and chomped for a moment. The sound of crunching made Evan hungry. "Those babies are as perfect as I knew they would be. Heads full of blond hair, adorable chubby cheeks. Little Charlie has your nose, and sweet Eva has my ears."

Evan lowered the armrest on the bed, climbing up to sit next to CeCe. Carefully, he tucked her to his side and kissed her temple. "Thank you," he whispered.

CeCe was incredulous. "For what? Struggling through ten hours of premature labor?"

"Well, yeah. But thank you for being you, for loving me, and for giving me the family I've always wanted."

CeCe's eyes brimmed with tears, but she blinked them away. She tried to tell her hormones to knock it off, but they wouldn't listen. "Not too bad for a geriatric pregnancy, huh?" She quipped, referring to the medical diagnosis that had nearly floored her. The Lawson's road to baby was long and winding, filled with painful moments that shook them to the core. However, it had also brought them where they were now, so no one was complaining. Rather, they were simply happy to be as fortunate as they were.

Evan chided, "Come on, babe. There is nothing geriatric about what I see." He reached down and took her hand, squeezing it firm until she reciprocated. His wife was a few years older, and Evan knew she blamed herself for the bumpy ride to pregnancy, but he wouldn't let her wallow. They were a team, and he'd share the weight of responsibility.

"Yeah, yeah. Forgive me if I don't believe you." She waggled her free hand, jostling the wires connected to the heart monitor. "This feels like something an old person needs."

"For the love of Pete," Mallory said from the doorway. She carried in a tray from the cafeteria, including herbal tea for CeCe and coffee for Evan. "Beckett and I were going to go, but not if I need to knock some sense into you."

Evan beamed at his sister. "Mal, you continue to impress me."

Beckett helped Mallory put the tray down before taking her hand and pulling her close. "She's the best."

CeCe scanned the tray and frowned. "Surely what I just did warrants a shot of something stronger than green tea?"

Mallory scoffed. "Nice try, Momma. I'll be the first one to pour you a shot when the time comes, which should be in about six months when you're done breastfeeding."

"Boo!" CeCe chanted, flopping her head back on her pillow. "But I'm in agony."

Evan pulled free of her grasp and jumped to his feet. "I'll get a nurse. How bad is the pain?" He frantically ran over to the wall where a helpful guide was tacked. It had ten smiley faces in a rainbow of colors and pain levels. "Are you a ten? Babe, are you a ten?" He stabbed the poster with his index finger, crinkling the paper.

Mallory snorted and shook with laughter. "Ev, don't ever change." She shrugged on her coat and gestured toward the door. "Beckett and I will leave you to it."

"Congratulations, Lawless," Beckett said, clapping his best friend on the back. "They're beautiful."

Evan flushed with pride. "Thanks, Foxy. They are, aren't they?"

CeCe rolled her eyes playfully. "Do I at least get an honorable mention?"

Mallory strode over and kissed CeCe on the forehead. "They are stunning, and you're one impressive Momma. You managed to eat an entire Christmas dinner while in labor. If that doesn't set those two up for success, nothing will."

"Hey, I'm a chef. Food is kind of my thing." She winked. Just as Mallory turned to go, CeCe reached out and took her hand. "Thank you, for everything. I know I'm not the best patient, but we're okay because of you."

Mallory blinked away the praise. "Anytime." On her way out, she hugged her brother and whispered, "You can get her something to eat if she gets hungry. Just don't let her go crazy."

"Love you, Mal."

"Love you more, Ev. Text when you need us."

Beckett waved, closing the door behind them with a quiet snick.

Evan nestled back onto the bed with CeCe in his arms. He wasn't in the most comfortable position, but he was hardly about to keep space between him and his wife. "Two little Christmas miracles." He sighed.

CeCe rested her head on his shoulder. "We did good."

"We did great."

They lay like that for an hour, staring into space and listening to the faint tune of Christmas carols piped through the hospital's hallway speakers. One of the nurses interrupted their quiet time as she rolled in the twins.

Charlie's blue hat was already loose, showing a puff of blond hair like his father's. Eva's cheeks were as rosy as the bow in her blonde curls, her cheeks plumped in a smile. "She's already smiling, look, babe." Evan held Eva up to CeCe.

The nurse muttered, "That might be gas," but no one heard her.

"Mrs. Lawson, did you want to try breastfeeding?" the other nurse asked.

CeCe sat up, adjusting her pillows. "No better time than the present."

Evan stepped back with Eva while Charlie got settled with CeCe. His lip trembled at the sight: the woman he loved more than life with the two people he would die for. These little wonders had already captured his heart, and he couldn't stand the level of happiness surging through him.

Once the nurses left and the babies were fed, Evan sat next to CeCe with Charlie, his tiny head resting on Evan's shoulder. "You doing okay?" he asked as CeCe's eyes drooped with fatigue.

"I'm perfect," she hummed, patting Eva's back until she let out the cutest belch either had ever heard. "Thank you," CeCe said, eyes fluttering closed.

"For what?"

"For asking me out ten years ago, for marrying me, for starting a bakery together, for staying by my side during all the IVF treatments, and for all the bottles you're going to be making in the very near future." Her lips quirked.

Evan adjusted Charlie so he could reach out for CeCe's hand. Being mindful of the wires, he held her hand and hoped she could sense how happy he was; how much joy radiated out of every pore.

"I would say anytime, but I think two children will be plenty."

"Agreed."

As she dozed, CeCe hummed along with the tune of *Silent Night*. Evan closed his own eyes, falling into the moment and reveling that his family—his life—was complete. He'd gotten everything and more for Christmas this year, and he knew he was the luckiest man in Buckeye Falls.

LIBBY KAY

CHAPTER 14
Same time next year?

"I don't think I've ever been this tired in my whole life," Ginny lamented, draining the last of her glass of champagne.

Natalie's stockinged feet rested on the table, her own glass of bubbly nestled against her chest. "Imagine how poor CeCe feels," she quipped, letting out a sigh and wiggling her toes.

Max and Anthony were at the counter, each nursing a beer, their eyes heavy and tired. Madeline drove Otis, Henry, and Josie home as soon as the baby drama began, and all four parents were relieved to have a moment of peace. Harold and Mona attempted to keep Maybelle forever, but sadly her parents wanted her home.

"I know Evan said they were covered with food, but there's so many leftovers. Should we go back and bring by some things?" Max asked, his gaze locking on the stacks of to-go boxes loaded with food.

Anthony rubbed his eyes, shoulders slumping forward. "I can swing by tomorrow with some things. You cooked, Max. The least I can do is play delivery driver."

Natalie, being Natalie, took charge of the situation.

"Those three aren't getting discharged from the hospital tomorrow, and I'm guessing Evan is up to his eyeballs with everything. Why don't we do what CeCe asked and *wait* to hear what they need?"

Ginny gestured her approval with her empty glass. "I'm with Nat. The last thing we want to do is be in the way."

"Are you sure?" Max asked Anthony.

Before Anthony could reply, his wife helpfully reminded him, "Do you remember when we had Otis? What was the last thing either of us wanted?"

Anthony snorted. "To see anyone who wasn't a combination of our DNA?"

Natalie snapped her fingers. "Bingo. Let them catch their breath, and we'll be ready."

Ginny clicked away on her phone for a moment, her fingers flying across the screen. A minute later, everyone's phones dinged. "There we go." She beamed.

Pulling out his phone, Max read through his texts. "What's up with this spreadsheet?"

Anthony tugged his phone from his jacket pocket and scoffed when he saw it. "I'm only disappointed my wife didn't come up with this first." He winked at Natalie, who flipped him the bird.

"Excuse me, but Gin's my business partner. If she did it, it's the same as me doing it." She winked at Ginny.

Max strode over to Ginny, looping his arms around her shoulders and pulling her close to his chest. "You're a dynamo, and I love it."

Ginny wiggled into his arms and sighed. "It's nothing they wouldn't do for us. We'll come up with a meal schedule to get them through the first few weeks. Then when their freezer is bursting and they can't stand the sight of other people, we'll retreat to our corners again."

Natalie filled out the first night, offering to make her famous chili. Anthony rubbed the back of his neck and asked, "Do you think they need anything that's not food? We still have some of O's bath toys and onesies."

Max nodded. "I know we still have Hen's toddler stuff, and of course there's Josie's …" He was stopped by Ginny covering his mouth with her hand.

"You're both sweet and very eager, but these babies are barely a day old. Why don't we save toys and clothes for a few months from now?"

Both men looked at each other with matching expressions of *What did we do?*

"You know what would be helpful," Natalie suggested, pulling herself to her feet and sliding her shoes back on. She briefly turned to the window and shuddered at the fat snowflakes that still fell. "You guys should finish boxing up the leftovers. We can drop them off at the shelter on our way home."

Ginny pointed to Natalie's feet, more crucially her sky-high heels. "You can't wear those outside. Not only will you slip and break your neck, but you'll freeze to death."

Max gestured toward his office in the back. "I know I have an extra pair of CeCe's work shoes if you want to wear those home."

Natalie was aghast, motioning at her perfectly coordinated outfit. It was festive yet formal, just like the woman herself. "Um, no, thank you. I'd risk losing a toe in this snow if it doesn't mess with the look."

Anthony walked up, bent his knees, and tossed Natalie over his shoulder in a fireman's hold. "Max, get those boxes ready for the shelter. I'll drop the missus in the car and double back." He swatted Natalie's behind as he strode out the door.

Ginny covered her mouth, attempting to hold in her laughter. Not only was Natalie fuming, but Anthony had every right to protect her ankles. "I'll help," she offered Max as they went to the kitchen and carried out enough food to feed an army.

Joining Anthony and Natalie at their SUV, they loaded up the boxes and sighed. "What a day," Ginny muttered. "I didn't even cook, and I'm exhausted." She ducked her head in the car and said, "Please thank Maddie for taking Hen and Josie home."

"Of course. What's the point of testing out Maddie's newfound driving skills?" Natalie quipped.

Anthony groaned. "Way to put our friends at ease. You make it sound like Maddie will be driving them off a cliff."

Natalie flapped a manicured hand. "Honey, it's Buckeye Falls. I don't think we have any cliffs."

"Text if you hear anything from CeCe and Evan, will you?" Max asked, slamming the trunk shut.

"You do the same." Anthony shot a thumbs-up while putting the car in reverse.

"Merry Christmas!" Ginny and Natalie shouted in unison.

"We'll have to do this every year," Natalie urged.

Ginny nodded, but couldn't hold back a scoff. "Yes, but maybe without the early labor and half the town showing up?"

"Deal," Anthony said, waving before driving down Main Street.

Max pulled Ginny close as they watched their friends drive away. Maybe it was the holiday putting him in a sentimental mood, but Max's eyes began to water. They had all come so far, and he sometimes couldn't believe it.

Misunderstanding, Ginny pulled back and sighed. "Max, the kids are home safe. I got a text from Josie an hour ago."

Dabbing at his cheeks with his sleeve, he let out a shuddering breath. "I know that. I just can't believe how much has changed."

"How so?" she asked, turning them toward the diner.

Max held the door open as they stepped into the kitchen, still warm from a day of the ovens working overtime.

Everyone had helped with cleaning up, so the only thing remaining was a box of leftover cheesy bites at CeCe's workstation. Max took the box and tucked it under his arm, clicking off the lights as he reached for his coat.

"I remember when you came back to town." Ginny's

shoulders tensed at the reminder of their time before reconciliation. "Anthony and I could hardly be in the same room with each other, and Evan followed CeCe around like a lovesick puppy."

Ginny softened, wrapping a scarf around her neck. "Well, Evan still follows CeCe around like a lovesick puppy."

"Okay, fair point. But look at how well everything turned out. We're back together—"

Ginny cut him off, kissing him briefly, and saying, "And happier than ever."

"Agreed," Max said on a sigh. "And now we're all paired off with families and careers and life. It's just, I don't know, amazing."

Ginny nodded, taking his hand and stepping back into the chilly Christmas night. "It is amazing, and I'd like to show you how amazing once we're back at home." She winked and strode to their car, an extra sway in her hips.

Max ran to catch up, tossing the box of crackers in the backseat and turning on the car. They made it home in record time. Thank goodness Buckeye Falls isn't known for its late-night traffic.

EPILOGUE
Ten years later

"You think they'll all make it?" Anthony asked, fidgeting with his tie. He ran his hands through his gray hair for the millionth time, earning an eye roll from his wife.

Natalie swatted his hand away, smoothing the lapels of his suit and straightening his tie. "Now, honey, you're going to mess up this outfit that I took a lot of time to perfect." She kissed his cheek before wiping away the lipstick smear. "They will all be here. You need to relax."

"Traffic in DC is no picnic on a good day, but at Christmas." Anthony shook his head and started pacing the room, nearly wearing the carpeting out. His wingtips slapped the floor in pace with his racing heart.

The doorbell rang, causing Anthony to jump. "Someone's here!" he exclaimed, barreling past his wife to get to the door.

"Just like I said," Natalie teased him. Even in her sky-high heels, she caught up to him.

When they opened the door, they were greeted to a sight that brought tears to their eyes. "Merry Christmas!" the gang cheered, filling their porch and spilling out onto the sidewalk.

Alice pushed through first, throwing her arm around her brother's waist. "Merry Christmas, Senator."

"Merry Christmas, Alice." Anthony held his sister tight, savoring the moment of peace. "And thanks for not calling me *Tony*."

Alice pulled back and rolled her eyes. "Spoiler alert, that will happen. I'm just being nice until you start feeding me."

James followed her inside, hugging Natalie and shaking Anthony's hand. "Big city politics look good on you, Anthony. Aren't politicians supposed to get surlier and more haggard?"

"And here I thought you were the good in-law," Natalie quipped, hip-checking James out of the way for the next round of guests.

"Sorry we're late," Beckett said, holding the door for Mallory and Maybelle. Both of whom had matching braids and red-and-green dresses. Beckett's genes had won out, and his daughter's hair was the color of a campfire, bold and fiery. "I forgot how to drive in a major city, apparently. I went through a roundabout three times before I could figure out our turn." He huffed, cheeks tinged with embarrassment.

Maybelle raised her hand. "I almost puked."

Mallory covered her daughter's mouth and pushed further into the house. "Ignore her, she's fine."

"Make way," CeCe said, leading a parade of her clan. The twins were at her heels, their blonde heads bobbing up the steps. Evan followed closely behind, carrying a tower of to-go boxes.

"If I tell you there's cheesy bites in here, will you hold the door?" Evan asked, shoulders slumping from the weight of the parcels.

"Only if that's the truth," Natalie said, helping Evan with his boxes before pulling CeCe into a bone-crushing hug.

Everyone filed into the kitchen and living room, the kids turning on the TV and entertaining themselves. Anthony craned his neck from the threshold and sighed. "I thought

Max and Ginny were going to make it."

Despite their best efforts, this would be their first Christmas together since the twins were born. Everyone was busy, the kids older and in some cases in college. Anthony and Natalie had left Buckeye Falls a year ago when he was elected to the US Senate. While they would still spend time in their family home, most of his efforts were focused in DC. Natalie had taken to their new roles with gusto, turning over most of her duties to Ginny and Madeline, who kept N&G afloat.

"Hold the door, Senator!" Max shouted from the sidewalk. He waved like a lunatic before bounding up the stairs and crushing Anthony in a hug. "Man, it's good to see you."

Anthony choked up, realizing just how relieved he was that everyone was there. Ginny's footsteps carried up the walkway until she joined in their group hug. "It's so good to see you."

"Ahhh!!!" Natalie squealed from behind them, tossing her arms around the growing group. "The fun can begin now."

Henry pushed past the parental reunion, eyes darting over the crowd. "Is O here?"

"What's up, man!" Otis said, joining his friend and bumping fists. "Want to see my new PlayStation?" And with that, the boys were entertained and out of the way.

"It's a shame that Maddie and Josie are so busy," Ginny lamented as she took off her coat. Natalie took it, draping it over her arm before dragging her friend down the hall to the coat closet. "I know Josie's at OSU and happy as a clam, but that doesn't mean I don't want her here."

Natalie made a sympathetic noise, the sound of a mother missing her children. "I'm still in shock that Maddie's boyfriend invited her to Christmas. It's too soon for that, right?"

Ginny bit her lip to keep from smiling. "Nat, she's twenty-six. She's been dating Colin for over a year. I'd say the timing is perfect."

CeCe stuck her head in the closet door, her eyes narrowing. "Are you having a special meeting already? I thought I'd at least have time to pop a cork and open the cheesy bites."

Before Ginny and Natalie could make room in the tiny space, CeCe was pushed in by Alice and Mallory. "Is this where the girls are hanging out?" Mallory asked over Alice's shoulder.

Alice scrunched her nose as a hanger hit her in the cheek. "I thought a senator's house would offer more of a seating area. Ouch," she exclaimed, rubbing her arm where Mallory had just pinched her.

"Everyone out!" Natalie said through the scarf in her mouth. Her heels wobbled as she gently shoved her friends out of the way. "We are headed to the kitchen where we can all sit and gossip in comfort."

While the wives paraded past the living room, finding Eva, Charlie, and Maybelle watching Christmas movies, they stumbled on the men in the kitchen. "Hey, this was supposed to be our turf," Natalie protested, getting on tiptoes to kiss Anthony's cheek.

Max waved a spatula from the stove, already clad in an apron. "Sorry, Nat. I wanted to get these sauces on the stove before anything got funky."

Ginny knelt to a tote bag on the floor, pulling out various canisters and boxes. "Please tell me the kids haven't gotten into the cookies already. I thought they were packed with the vegetables?"

Anthony cupped his hands in front of his mouth and bellowed, "O! Where are the cookies?"

A moment later, Otis and Henry shuffled into the kitchen with guilty expressions. Ginny put her hands on her hips and sighed. "Hen, we've been here ten minutes. How could you have already eaten the cookies?"

Even in his late teens, their son was still a little troublemaker. He dusted crumbs from his ugly Christmas sweater and sighed. "Mom, we were in the car for hours. You couldn't expect me to hold off the whole time."

Max stifled a laugh. "Did you at least save some for the group?"

Now it was Otis's turn in the hot seat. He surreptitiously wiped a smudge of chocolate from the corner of his lips. "I assure you, Hen did share with the group."

Everyone laughed, and CeCe held up her hand. "I think I can salvage this." She turned to Evan and asked, "Where was our box of cookies and cheesy bites?"

"In here, Mom!" Charlie shouted from the living room.

Evan snorted. "Then I guess we're skipping dessert, because those rascals will eat anything that isn't nailed down."

"Oh man, I wanted some of those," Otis said, following Henry to the living room with the rest of the kids.

"Good thing I made an apple crisp," Beckett said, earning a cheer from Evan.

Natalie shrugged. "Crisis averted. Now, whose drinking?"

Two hours later, everyone was seated for their first Christmas together in years. The kids were relegated to the living room, smushed together around a folding card table. The adults surrounded the dining room table with barely enough space for their plates. The cramped quarters didn't matter though, because the food—and company—was amazing.

Max and CeCe glazed a ham that was fit for the cover of a magazine, while Natalie, Ginny, Mallory, and Evan handled the side dishes. Alice and James were not needed for their decoration skills, because Natalie had hired a professional decorator. She gave the White House a run for its money on tasteful, classy décor. Beckett attempted to play bartender, but he lacked the flair and finesse of Chloe and Addison.

"I'm still disappointed Chloe and Addy couldn't make it." Alice sighed as Beckett poured her a cocktail he made on the fly. Fortunately no one winced at the odd flavor combinations of cranberry and juniper.

James took her free hand and squeezed. "I know, but they're busy at their place." True to her dream, Chloe got a quiet place outside New York with Addison. While the city was still important to them, both women now had the space to relax and enjoy their time together. Less hustle, but all heart.

"Hey, Uncle Beckett, can I have a beer?" Otis asked, already reaching out for a bottle.

Beckett flinched, glancing around the room for confirmation. Natalie let out a sigh from the tips of her toes. "It's okay, Beckett. O's sadly legal."

Henry held a hand in the air and grinned. "And I think I should be allowed to have one, too. You know, since it's Christmas."

Everyone burst out laughing, but Anthony gave in and handed him a beer. "You get one, and don't tell my constituents that I'm promoting underage drinking."

Otis and Henry darted back to the safety of the living room before Max and Ginny could change their mind.

Anthony raised his wine glass in a toast. "Now that everyone has a drink, I propose a toast!" he exclaimed, cheeks rosy from his earlier imbibing. "To friends that are like family, and to Buckeye Falls. Merry Christmas!"

"Merry Christmas," the group responded.

They didn't know what the new year would bring, but they knew they could handle anything together. Anthony's schedule only got busier the more he got involved in DC politics. Ginny and Madeline—when she wasn't working on her next art piece—were expanding N&G yet again, and Natalie pondered opening an East Coast office. Max was focused on the diner and Max's Gin Joint, which Henry was beginning to show interest in. Evan and CeCe were cooking and baking at both of Max's places, but they split their time at the bakery on Beckett and Mallory's farm. James had another show coming up in Europe in the spring, and one of Alice's books was being optioned for a Netflix special.

Everyone was thriving.

Everyone was in love.

Everyone was exactly where they were supposed to be … even if there weren't enough cheesy bites to go around.

LIBBY KAY

RECIPES FROM BUCKEYE FALLS

Author's note:

If you've enjoyed this series, and I hope you have, you'll see my love of food throughout each story. Whether the characters are cooking for each other or sharing a greasy takeout burger, food is instrumental in bringing people together—and in a lot of ways showing their love.

The following recipes are just a few of my favorites from the series. Admittedly, a few of the confections described in the books are well beyond my culinary prowess. We'll leave the real baking to CeCe. 😊

Happy cooking and baking, readers. I hope you enjoy this taste of Buckeye Falls.

Max's Cheese Enchiladas

Prep: 15 minutes

Cook: 30 minutes.

Ingredients:

For the enchiladas:

- Small corn tortillas
- 2 small cans of green enchilada sauce
- 3 cups of shredded cheese—like Colby Jack, Pepper Jack, or Cheddar
- 1 teaspoon ground cumin
- 1 teaspoon of garlic powder
- Salt and pepper to taste

Toppings:

- Sour cream
- Diced avocado
- Scallions
- Pickled jalapenos—if you like it spicy

Directions:

- Preheat oven to 350 degrees.
- Grease a 9 x13 casserole dish.
- Combine the sauce and seasonings in a bowl.

- Pour a small amount of enchilada sauce on the bottom of the dish.

- Take each tortilla, fill with a small handful of cheese, and roll up. Nestle together in the pan.

- When the pan is filled with tortillas, pour over the sauce mixture and any remaining cheese.

- Bake uncovered for 30 minutes, until the whole dish is bubbling and the cheese is golden brown.

- Let sit 5 minutes before serving.

- Serve with desired toppings.

- Serves 6 to 8

CeCe's Famous Cheesy Bites

Prep: 10 to 15 minutes—plus chilling time

Bake: 20 to 25 minutes

Ingredients:

- 1 stick of salted butter, at room temperature
- 1 and ¼ cups of parmesan cheese (I use the stuff in the green canister.)
- ½ teaspoon of kosher salt
- ½ teaspoon of black pepper
- 1 and ¼ cups of flour
- 2-3 tablespoons of heavy cream
- Optional – 1 teaspoon of dried thyme or herbs de. Provence

Directions:

- Either with a mixer or a wooden spoon, cream the butter until it's slightly whipped and smooth.
- Add the parmesan, salt, pepper, and herbs. Mix together until it's a uniform mixture.
- Slowly add the flour until it's combined. The mixture should be a little clumpy.

- Add the heavy cream, starting with 2 tablespoons. The dough just needs to form together, but not be wet or sticky.

- Pour the dough onto a large piece of plastic wrap and form a log shape, approximately 9 inches to a foot long. Put the dough in the fridge for at least an hour, but up to 48 hours works.

- When ready to bake, preheat the oven to 350 degrees. Line your baking sheet with parchment paper and slice the dough into disks. Place one inch apart on the tray.

- Bake for 20 - 25 minutes. The bites should be golden on the bottom and pale on top.

- Let cool and serve. They are great with fruit or other cheeses, or as a solo snack.

- Makes approximately 20 crackers.

Max's Christmas Morning Breakfast Casserole

Prep: 20 minutes—plus chilling time

Cook: 60 minutes

Ingredients:

- 2 cups 2% milk
- 6 eggs, beaten
- 2 cups of shredded cheddar cheese (I add an extra half cup for the holidays.)
- 8 slices of white or wheat bread—pre-sliced from the grocery store. (The fancy stuff won't work here.)
- Butter—enough for the pan and the bread (Usually half a stick)
- 1 pound of bulk sausage—either Italian or breakfast sausage
- Salt and pepper to taste

Directions:

- Grease a 9x13 glass pan, set aside.
- Cook sausage, draining excess fat. Set aside to cool while you prep the rest of the casserole.
- Butter one side of each slice of bread. Lay butter side down in the pan, covering both the bottom of the pan

and the sides. (You will have to play Tetris and trim the bread to make it fit.)

- Sprinkle the cooked sausage all over the bread.
- Beat the eggs, milk, salt and pepper together. Pour over the bread and sausage.
- Grate the cheese and sprinkle over the finished casserole.
- Cover the pan in foil and refrigerate overnight. (Up to 24 hours in advance.)
- The next morning, preheat oven to 350 degrees. Bake the casserole covered for 45 minutes. Remove foil and bake for another 15 to 20 minutes, until the top is golden and the eggs are set.
- Let sit for 5 minutes before slicing.
- Serves 6 to 8

Note: If you're not a sausage fan, diced ham is an excellent substitute.

Natalie's Chili

Prep: 25 minutes

Cook 60 minutes, but can simmer for hours

Ingredients:

For the chili:

- 1 pound ground beef (substitute ground turkey for a lower-fat version)
- 1 can dark red kidney beans (rinsed and drained)
- 1 can light red kidney beans (rinsed and drained)
- 1 can black beans (rinsed and drained)
- 1 can pinto beans (rinsed and drained)
- 1 large onion
- 1 green bell pepper
- 1 yellow bell pepper (I like the color, but any other bell pepper will do.)
- 1 can (15 oz) diced tomatoes (do NOT drain)
- 1 can beer
- Chili powder (1 to 3 tablespoons depending on desired heat)
- 1 tablespoon smoked paprika
- 1 tablespoon cumin
- Salt and red pepper flakes to taste.
- Optional: Add a can of drained corn.

Topping options:

- Corn chips
- Sour cream
- Shredded cheese
- Scallions
- Pickled jalapeños
- Sliced avocado
- Fresh chopped cilantro

Directions:

- In a Dutch oven or sturdy stock pot, brown the ground meat.
- Add the diced onion and peppers, cook until tender, about 10 minutes.
- Add the spices, cooking a moment before adding the liquids.
- Pour in the beer and undrained can of tomatoes. Mix and let simmer covered for at least 15 minutes before adding beans.
- Add the beans (and corn if using), stir and cover. Let simmer at least 30 minutes. This gets better the longer it cooks. (You can make it the day before if you'd like.)
- Serve with desired toppings.
- Serves 6 to 10

Beckett's Apple Crisp

Prep: 15 minutes

Bake: 40 to 50 minutes

Ingredients:

For the base:

- 6 large green apples, peeled and sliced
- 2 sweet red apples, like Gala or Honeycrisp, peeled and sliced
- 1 small orange—juiced
- 4 tablespoons flour
- ¼ cup of granulated sugar
- 1 teaspoon cinnamon
- Pinch of nutmeg (optional)

For the crisp topping:

- 1 cup of flour
- 1 and ½ cups of oatmeal (quick cook oats are fine)
- ¾ cup of brown sugar
- ½ cup of granulated sugar
- Pinch of salt
- 1 and a half sticks of butter, diced into cubes (if you use salted, skip the pinch of salt)
- 1 teaspoon cinnamon

Directions:

- Preheat oven to 350 degrees. Lightly grease a 9 x13 casserole dish.

- In a mixing bowl, combine the sliced apples, 1 teaspoon of cinnamon, 4 tablespoons of flour, ¼ cup of sugar, and juice from the orange. Pour this combination into the waiting casserole dish.

- Using the same bowl, combine all the crisp ingredients. I prefer using my hands, but a wooden spoon or pastry blender work, too. The mixture will clump together when it's ready.

- Crumble the topping over the fruit mixture, ensuring the whole dish is covered in crisp.

- Bake for 40 - 50 minutes uncovered, until there are bubbles throughout the crisp.

- Let cool slightly and serve with whipped cream or a scoop of vanilla ice cream.

ACKNOWLEDGEMENTS

These acknowledgments are a little bittersweet to write. Writing the Buckeye Falls series has been a dream from start to finish. I could not have done it without the wonderful folks at Inkspell Publishing. To Melissa, thank you for taking a chance on me and my books. I will always appreciate your kindness, support, and dedication to the series ... and me! I'd also like to thank Yeza for another wonderful job editing the nonsense that is my first drafts. You're the best.

One of the great features of Inkspell is the family of authors. Thank you for your support and encouragement as we put our words out into the world. I couldn't navigate my writing journey without all of you.

Next, to my podcasting partner in crime, Liz Donatelli. Thank you for picking me as your Romance RoundUp co-host ... Every recording truly is a blast. It is a dream talking all things romance with you, and I look forward to the episodes and events to come. Giddy up! 😀

A writer is only as good as the friends who listen to her rant and rave. To Thelma, Ernie, and the Jets. I love you all and could not fathom a world without your support, memes, and laughs.

To my parents, sister, and family who continue to brag about my writing journey and share in the stumbles and triumphs. Love you all to pieces!

To the readers that found this series and love the residents of Buckeye Falls as much as I do. Your support and enthusiasm make this wild writing journey worthwhile. I hope you loved the end of the series, and I hope you'll follow me onto the next writing adventure. I promise I'll make it swoon-worthy. ♥

Last, and certainly never least, to my husband. My life is filled with love because of you, and I cherish your support, your smile, and your sense of humor. I love you, Curly. Thanks for joining me on this writing dream.

DON'T MISS ANOTHER BUCKEYE FALLS STORY

Falling Home

Welcome to Buckeye Falls, Ohio!
'Tis the Season for Second Chances...And this couple is going to need a Christmas Miracle!

When New York transplant Ginny Meyer returns to her small hometown to help her father recover from surgery, she isn't looking for any complications. No Christmas caroling, no cookie decorating, and certainly no time spent with her ex-husband, Max. The trouble is, she's looped into helping with the Christmas Jubilee—and a certain ex is her planning partner. Now all her plans to avoid Max disappear in a puff of tinsel. But she can resist his charms, right?

Max Sanchez has three great loves in his life—his diner, Christmas, and his ex-wife. He's spent two years missing the woman who broke his heart and left town, and he'll use any excuse to spend time with her. Max hopes some holiday cheer, and his famous cheese enchiladas, can help them find their way back together. Buckeye Falls hasn't felt the same since Ginny left, and Max can tell she's warming to the idea of staying in town. Now if only he could get her to stay with him…

With a little help from the residents of Buckeye Falls, this Christmas is bringing more than presents under the tree.

Author Libby Kay's books are perfect for fans of Kristan Higgins' second chance romances or Sharon Sala's smalltown romances. Readers will fall in love with Buckeye Falls, Ohio and the townspeople as they embrace the holiday season. Slip in to this enchanting smalltown and stay awhile! You might just fall in love…

EXCERPT:

Blinking, Ginny begged her eyes to see someone else standing before her. It was as if her memories willed themselves back to life. Beside her, her father perked up and lifted his free hand. "Max, over here." Max turned around, and Ginny felt the air leave her lungs. This was no trick of her mind. It was the real deal. *Well, hell …*

Time had been good to Max; there was no denying it. His dark hair was longer now, curling at the base of his neck. A few flecks of gray threatened to take over his temples, but he managed to look mature rather than haggard. Instead of the clean-shaven face she remembered, his chiseled jawline was now peppered with a few days of stubble. Suddenly, Ginny understood all the fuss with lumbersexuals.

Max's brown eyes darkened when he saw her, but his steps didn't falter. "Harold, good to see you." He moved one of his shopping bags to his other arm and shook her father's hand. When he turned to her, Ginny felt her breath hitch as he reached out his hand for a shake. *Really? They were in the hand-shaking phase of their relationship?*

Ginny reached out and took his hand, a shot of awareness coursing through her body as his fingers wrapped around hers. "Max," she said his name in greeting, hoping her tone was light, carefree.

"Gin." Max swallowed and squeezed her hand before letting it go. He didn't say anything at first, just studied her. She was glad she had listened to her father about makeup. Bumping into her ex-husband with bedhead and sans mascara would have been mortifying.

Ginny was helpless for a moment, staring at Max like a fool.

Perhaps she'd fallen into an alternate universe when she left the turnpike? Maybe her rental car was a time machine where she felt pulled to a man who bruised her heart? A man whose heart was certainly broken by her.

Either oblivious or uncaring of her current slack-jawed state, Max surprised her by stepping closer and giving her a genuine smile. "I'm glad you're back," he said. "It's really good to see you."

In that moment, staring into his warm gaze, Ginny couldn't disagree. Being so close to Max, so close to the worn paths of their past, she felt comfortable. This didn't feel like a foreign place; it felt like home.

Falling For You

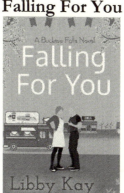

Welcome to Buckeye Falls, Ohio!
Sparks fly in this small town as everyone's favorite gruff pastry chef finally gives the sweetest guy in town a chance.

CeCe LaRue knows what she wants in life, and in the kitchen, and that's control. She doesn't have time for distractions—from her past or present. But that doesn't mean a certain bright-eyed coworker hasn't captured her heart.

Evan Lawson is a chronic optimist, and he brings his sunny disposition to everything he does, especially his job at the diner. It's obvious why he loves his job so much, and it has everything to do with CeCe. He's been crushing on her for a while, but he's biding his time. Much like the perfect recipe, love cannot be rushed.

When a major food competition comes to town, Evan is thrilled at the prospect of competing. Despite her stellar culinary skills, CeCe is hesitant to participate. The celebrity chef host is more than a pretty face; he's the painful past she's been outrunning for years.

Can CeCe open herself up to the prospect of love and give Evan a chance? Can Evan's optimism keep them both afloat?

Falling For You is part of the Buckeye Falls series and can be enjoyed as a stand-alone read. Author Libby Kay's books are perfect for fans of Penny Reid and Sharon Sala's smalltown romances. These sweet romances will have readers falling in love with Buckeye Falls, Ohio. Slip in to this enchanting smalltown and stay awhile! You might just fall in love…

EXCERPT:

They were friends, friends with a whole lot of potential. Surely this magnetic pull wasn't one-sided?

"I think I could be serious about you," CeCe finally said, the words shaking Evan back to the moment. "And I don't know what to do about that."

Evan felt his heart explode in his chest. "You do?"

CeCe slowly raised her hand and cupped his cheek, having to stand on tiptoe to make up for their height difference. How easily he forgot her height when they were together. She was such a force, she filled up every space she was in. Her energy, her passion for what she did, radiated around her.

Even now, standing outside with only the din of the pub surrounding them, CeCe was all he could see, feel, and touch. Her thumb swiped around his lips, making him shiver. "I do."

Words escaping him, Evan closed the distance to kiss her. It was slow, tender. They were feeling each other out, finding the angles where they fit best. Cradling her face in his hands, the world around them evaporated. CeCe moaned, and Evan swallowed it, wanting to savor every little thing she gave him. Kissing CeCe felt crucial, like he'd die without her touch, die without having the privilege of her.

Falling Again

Welcome back to Buckeye Falls, Ohio!
Does this small town mayor have the political savvy to negotiate his way back into his wife's heart?

From the outside, Mayor Anthony Snyder and his wife Natalie have it all. Adorable children, a lovely home, and a never-ending supply of free food from the local diner. But behind closed doors, this duo struggles to stay connected. The sparkle they show Buckeye Falls has turned a little dull on the home front.

Over the last decade, things became hectic in the Snyder household. Anthony was elected to office, following in his father's footsteps. Unfortunately, he's reminded regularly that these are big shoes to fill. Being the best mayor takes a lot of time—time he's not spending with his family.

Natalie prides herself on being everything to everyone, but the job of a wife hasn't been smooth sailing. Wrapped up in her own growing business and their kids' activities, her time with Anthony has dwindled faster than her secret stash of Halloween candy. Natalie longs for quality time with the man she loves, but it never seems to be in the cards.

A chance to visit their family lake house promises a week away from it all, but can these two reconnect when there's no distractions? Or is it time for these high achievers to admit that love might be the one thing they can't master?

With a little help from the residents of Buckeye Falls, this power couple will find their way back to happily ever after.

Falling Again **is the third book in the Buckeye Falls series, but it can be enjoyed as a standalone read. Featuring similar marriage conflicts as in Lyssa Kay Adams'** *The Bromance Book Club* **and the small-town romance of Susan Mallery's** *Fool's Gold* **series, fans will love this second chance love story. After all, who doesn't deserve to fall in love again?**

EXCERPT:
"Anthony saw me topless, and vice versa, for the first time in ages yesterday."

Ginny raised an eyebrow. "Isn't that a good thing?"

"It would be if we'd done anything about it. Both times we were cleaning up after the kids and didn't even acknowledge it happened. Or I guess that it didn't happen."

Ginny paused, clearly unsure how to continue. "Has it been a while since you two—" she swirled her mug in the air, gesturing for Natalie to finish the sentence. Apparently, her friend wasn't going easy on her this morning.

"Had sex? Yes. It's been a while. It's been so long that I don't even remember the basic mechanics of the deed. And don't even ask me when it was. Sometime between Otis's conception and last Thursday." Natalie sank back in her chair and groaned. "This is bad."

*

Placing her hand over his mouth to shut him up, Natalie shook her head. "Stop that. You are a wonderful husband and father. Just because we hit a rough patch doesn't mean all the ways you love us don't shine through." Beneath her hand, Anthony sighed. He sounded so defeated; she wanted to wrap him in a blanket and hide him from the world. "I've made some mistakes too. You're not allowed to play the blame game alone. It's a two-player game."

Faking the Fall

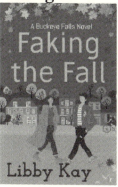

Sparks fly when a reclusive artist meets his muse in this new installment of the Buckeye Falls series.

Alice Snyder knows her reputation—and if she didn't, Buckeye Falls loves to remind her. She may come from the town's First Family, but that doesn't mean she plays by the rules. After a decade of traveling and going to school, she's back home and ready to settle down, or at least relax for a while. The trouble is, her neighbors are determined to find her a husband. She needs a way to get them off her back…

When James Gibson, a divorced artist, flees New York for the peace of small-town Ohio, he's excited to get painting again. The only trouble is, he's completely blocked. Despite his best efforts, his collection of canvases are blank and he's at a career crossroads. A chance meeting with the mayor's sister throws James's routine off balance, and he's eager to spend more time with this quirky spitfire.

And Alice might have the solution to both their problems…
Fake Date.

She gets the Nosey Nellies off her back, and James gets time with a woman who inspires him both *inside and outside* the studio.

Just a few weeks of pretending, and they'll move on. Simple, right? The trouble is the more time they spend together, the realer their relationship feels. The laughter, the stolen kisses—it all starts to feel like more.

Can these two be honest with each other and find their happily-ever-after, or are they doomed for a *real* breakup?

Libby Kay's FAKING THE FALL redeems Buckeye Falls's spinster troublemaker with a fake relationship romance filled with sweet small town vibes. FAKING THE FALL will bring to mind amazing books like Practice Makes Perfect by Sarah Adams and Fix Her Up by Tessa Bailey. But best of all, it returns readers to the small Ohio town and the familiar characters from the previous Buckeye Falls books. All the zany, overbearing, and well-meaning ones! So sit back and grab FAKING THE FALL for the latest roller-coaster romance by Libby Kay.

EXCERPT:

A lock of chocolatey hair had fallen from her ponytail. James lifted his hand and tucked the silky strands behind her ear. Her skin was as soft as rose petals, and he suddenly forgot this wasn't real. That this sweet woman standing in front of him wasn't his. James dipped his head and saw the moment Alice registered his intent. Her green eyes grew dark and her tongue poked out to moisten her bottom lip. There was no going back now.

"Alice." James croaked her name through the lump in his throat. He had to taste her, just once.

"Kiss me," she whispered.

She tasted like ginger—warm, spicy and inviting. James couldn't believe his luck that he was actually kissing Alice. His hands slid up to cup her cheek, cradling her against him. Their lips nipped at each other, curious yet hungry. He hadn't shared a kiss like that in far too long. The world around him burst into color— bold reds and sharp oranges.

Just when James was ready to deepen the kiss, Alice pulled back. Resting her hands on his chest, she sighed. "I think that worked," she said, her breathing labored.

"What?" James asked, struggling to clear his head.

Alice gestured over his shoulder. "Roxie and Jennie followed us out. I just wanted to make sure they—" But her explanation died on her tongue. James stepped back, his arms falling limp at his sides.

It was all for show. That moment of color and passion meant nothing to Alice. "I'll get you home," he said, keeping his gaze focused anywhere but on her.

Forever to Fall

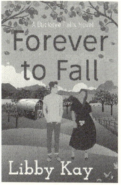

Welcome to Buckeye Falls, where second chances mend broken hearts for these childhood sweethearts. Wedding bells are ringing, but the sister of the groom is conflicted.

Fifteen years ago, Mallory Lawson "married" her childhood sweetheart, Beckett, in a pretend wedding on his family's apple farm. She treasures not only the memories, but the ring he put on her finger. The trouble now, her brother, Evan, wants to put that family heirloom on his fiancée's finger. Mallory adores CeCe, but she struggles to get past her girlhood fantasies of Beckett swooping back into her life with a certain ruby ring...

Beckett Fox is at a crossroads. After losing his grandfather, he's listless and fearful of coming back to the family farm. There are too many memories, and most of them are tied to the love of his life, Mallory. He doesn't even

LIBBY KAY

know if she remembers that fateful day when they were kids, playing make-believe under the apple trees, but he does. Now he's back to help his buddy get married, and he hopes to find peace on the family farm, with Mallory by his side…

When the wedding planning kicks into high gear, Beckett and Mallory are thrust together as maid of honor and best man. The more time they spend together, the harder it is to ignore the sparks between them. Beckett fears Evan won't support him dating Mallory, so the pair date in secret. But true love won't stay hidden forever…

Best-selling author Libby Kay's Buckeye Falls Series reminds readers of small-town life where everyone knows each other. Fans of Sharon Sala's *Blessings, Georgia* series and Susan Mallery's *Fool's Gold* series will fall in love with Buckeye Falls and the childhood sweethearts who are tired of hiding their feelings. Come for the wedding and stay for the whole series.

EXCERPT:

Rubbing the back of his neck, Beckett felt his muscles relax at her presence. Mallory had this amazing ability to calm him down while simultaneously causing him to burn with lust.

For a moment, neither of them spoke. The sound of cicadas in the night air surrounded them, their nightly song echoing through Buckeye Falls. Mallory finally cleared her throat and gestured with the box toward the door. "Can I come in?"

"Erm, yeah." Beckett stepped back and held the door open for her, catching a whiff of her perfume as she slunk inside. Mallory always smelled like summertime: sweet and tangy like a handful of blackberries.

Mallory took a few paces inside and looked around. Beckett said a silent prayer of thanks that he had the forethought to start unpacking. It was a mess, but at least it looked like his mess. "Cute." She said the word with a small smile, plopping the box on top of the coffee table.

She turned like she was going to leave, her presence not required beyond the delivery. Instinctively, Beckett blocked the way, letting the door close behind him on a soft click. "Where are you going?" he asked, his pulse kicking up at the idea that he wouldn't see her for more than another moment.

Shrugging, Mallory pointed to the door. "Home?"

Before he could think better of it, Beckett blurted out the first thing that came to mind. "Stay. Have dinner with me."

Mallory didn't respond at first, but he didn't miss the flush that crept up her neck. "You want to have dinner with me?"

"Yes?" he replied, although it was far from a question. Beckett wanted Mallory to stay as long as she liked—for dinner or the rest of her life. He wasn't picky.

Now Available In Ebook And Print Where Books Are Sold

ABOUT THE AUTHOR

Libby Kay lives in the city in the heart of the Midwest with her husband. When she's not writing, Libby loves reading romance novels of any kind. Stories of people falling in love nourish her soul. Contemporary or Regency, sweet or hot, as long as there is a happily ever after—she's in love!

When not surrounded by books, Libby can be found baking in her kitchen, binging true crime shows, or on the road with her husband, traveling as far as their bank account will allow.

Libby cohosts the Romance Roundup podcast with Liz Donatelli on the Reader Seeks Romance Channel where they recommend romance books and interview authors, influencers, and publishers. Check it out for your weekly dose of romance!

Website: https://www.libbykayauthor.com/

Instagram and Facebook: @LibbyKayAuthor
Goodreads: @LibbyKay

Made in the USA
Middletown, DE
17 December 2024

67472472R00104